The Great Escape

Memories of Tribal Violence

Andrew Maina

Published by Solano Publications
Email; solanopublications@gmail.com
Tel; 0727 553 440

Designed by I. Oluoch Otieno
Illustrated by Gilbert Gesora

First published 2020

ISBN 978 9966 955 93 7

Email; andrewmaina2010@yahoo.com
P.O. Box 3990, 01002
Thika, Kenya
Tel; 0721 518 616

Printed & Bound by
Tinta Image Communications
P.O. Box 13353
Nairobi.
Tel 0710 460 947
Email; fpcomm@gmail.com

Dedication

To my sister, the late Esther Wanjiku

Acknowledgments

My warm appreciation goes to Purity, my wife and to Selma, Samantha and Shayna, my daughters for their love and support during the writing and publication of this book. To Derek Schofield for his advice, suggestions and for reading the manuscript. To Kuria Muchiri, Gituma M'Ikiara and James Kamau for editing the manuscript, and to Tabitha for typing services.

Chapter One

"Will I ever go back to Kisumu?" I asked, bitter and not pleased with such a possibility.

No one answered though I was in the car with my brother, his wife, my mum and two sisters. Also in the car were my two nephews and our house help.

Omosh my brother and the third born in the family, was at the wheel and like a sphinx concentrated on the road ahead. What I couldn't tell was whether he heard my question or not. Sitting beside him and with the gear lever in between her thighs kondele kondele style was Pauline our house help.

Pauline was a girl of my age and on a normal day went about her work talking little, but very efficiently. Like my companions in the car, she said nothing and as a co-driver concentrated on the road ahead.

Like the other members of my family, I was heavily bodied and had been struggling with losing weight to a reasonable level. As such, piling us up in the car had been a delicate exercise at the start of the journey. However, picking Pauline to take the 'gear lever' seat had been easy for she was a slim girl who in her jeans and short, combed hair looked more like a boy.

Any girl taking such a seat right next to the wife of the driver could have been embarrassed whenever the gear was shifted. However, Pauline did not flinch and seemed not bothered by the seating arrangement. This was because she knew very well like everyone else in the car that the situation we were in had no place for such sentiments. Each of us was grateful that we were at least inside a moving car.

Next to Pauline was Daisy, wife to Omosh. Daisy sat with her head leaning on the head rest while holding their last born son on her lap. From where I sat, I could not see the baby but his frenzied suckling from time to time told of a failed attempt in dislodging the nipple from his mouth. I even imagined that one of his small hands clung onto the remaining breast protectively. This was her favourite suckling mode.

Defeated, Daisy sat dozing and completely resigned to the tyranny of the little boy who owned that part of her body. She too pretended not to have heard my question.

The other person in the car was Wanjiku my mother, who the grandchildren simply called *shosh*. The point at which she became a cucu, (a grandmother, digitized into *shosh*) to everyone in the family I can't tell but there she sat beside me, calm as if nothing monstrous was happening to her family. Currently, she was engaged in a game with one of her grandsons and looked very much like a grandmother accompanying her family on a holiday. I can swear that she had perfectly heard my question but from what I knew about her, chose not to comment.

"*Shosh shosh* look at this," Denis a boy of five and son to my sister Petronila drew the attention of shosh.

They lived in Nairobi and had come to Kisumu for the Christmas holidays.

Using a piece of tissue paper, the boy had made an impressive figure of a boat. Held on one end, it smoothly sailed in the little space between us. What worried me was what could happen if it ever landed in water. He conducted his boat construction business while comfortably sitting on his mother's lap.

Other than Denis, the boat maker, Petronila had a daughter who was slightly younger than I was. Leah was her name and like Pauline was a slim girl. While I struggled with my weight, Leah was a different story. She had a healthy appetite and ate and ate without worry. We used to tease her that she ate like an ant and yet had nothing to show for it. I still wonder where all the food she ate went.

She too did not respond to my question but sat quietly sandwiched between the heavy weights in the family, Shosh and Joy. Joy was our eldest sister and the sixth person in the car. Like all the other passengers, Joy also said nothing but I was not bothered.

While I was disappointed by the manner in which my question had been ignored by my fellow passengers, I was in fact relieved that Joy had said nothing. This was because any comment from her concerning our future, or anything to do with Kisumu, the city we were fleeing from could have drawn a torrent of tears which we all dreaded. All she needed was a small trigger and all the pains from her experiences in the last twenty four hours would be stirred. They had been horrifying experiences and we all worried over her health.

Even by Kisumu standards, our car, a Toyota Corolla saloon was overloaded and could have put to shame the Peugeot 404 Kondele Kondele taxis. This is because a Toyota Corolla cannot be compared with a Peugeot 404 saloon in size and cramming six people and two children in such a space was only possible in extremely desperate circumstances.

Among these five women passengers in the car, three could comfortably stand among the PPCE Woman's Guild Members. A PPCE Woman's Guild Member can simply be described as a well-fed woman with ample hips. She is also a nightmare to any Matatu conductor hoping to seat five adults on a seat meant for three.

When coaxing passengers to move a bit and create space for an extra person on a seat meant for three but already holding four, matatu conductors were fond of using their past experiences of packing on the same space five PPCE Woman's Guild Members.

Our car was not only loaded with six adults but also another young man who was our cousin and a student at Maseno University. He was a son to one of my many paternal aunties and worked as a waiter in our restaurant during the holidays. He also lived with us during such periods.

Like a bird or even a rat making a home, he had lined the boot of the car with some of our clothes, and made himself a nest in which he had folded himself. Any extra space he did not desperately need had been filled with bags and paper bags containing our belongings. The overloaded boot was held in place by a rope. This also ensured that the 'nester' had enough supply of air.

Despite his cramped travelling position, Victor, for that was his name was grateful that he too was in the car although in its boot. His only complaint was the intermittent ouch we heard whenever the car hit a pothole.

Though technically in the car, I did not expect an answer from Victor and I even doubted that he could have followed our conversation. With no one keen on answering my question, I left it hanging in the little space of the stuffy-hot-overloaded car and looked without seeing, the scenery outside.

Meanwhile, our car which was crammed with passengers in its cabin and in its boot, while its carrier was piled high with suitcases and some of the things we could not leave behind, flew over the potholes despite the many 'ouches' from the boot. In a normal day, we could not have gone beyond the Nyamasaria police road block without 'talking well' with the traffic police officers.

"Show it to Aunt Becky," Joy told the boat builder. Everybody called me Becky though my name is Rebecca Anyango Otieno.

Joy, our oldest sister was supposed to be a joyful woman as her name suggested but she wasn't, especially this morning. She wore a grave face that was not only a complete contradiction to what her name meant but an abuse to the rich imaginative naming process of my parents. With her grave face, I had this funny feeling that she should have been given a name that was 'all mood swings compliant'. Such was her current mood that attempts in drawing her into our conversation had been useless. She simply sat and allowed the boy romp on her lap with her mind miles away.

I truly felt sorry for Joy. Anyone with a heart could. She had lost her husband a year ago and with her three children, two boys and a girl, away in the U.S.A, lived alone in what 24 hours ago had been an immaculate cottage in Manyatta Estate. That was until a gang latched both her front and rear doors from the outside, and through a broken window pane splashed petrol into her sitting room.

"Can you smell that," the gang leader had shouted through the now broken window in her sitting room. It was as if he had thrown a bouquet of roses in front of her nose.

What she smelled was not the sweet fragrance of roses but an alarm raising smell, the smell of petrol. "I can smell it but please do not burn the house. I will give you whatever you want," my sister hiding behind the slightly open door to the sitting room pleaded in panic.

"Open the door then and stop wasting our time," the spokesman ordered with impatience. Though ready to give them everything, Joy was still reluctant in letting the gang into her house.

"This is the last time I am asking you. Open the door or I throw this inside," the gang leader threatened, holding a burning match stick in his hand. With shaking hands, Joy opened the door and in less than a minute the house was stripped bare of anything they thought was of value.

"Give us the money," one of the thugs holding her hand and leading her to the bedroom demanded.

Long before she opened the front door, she had grabbed her purse from the bedroom and hoped that in offering it, the gang would take whatever else they wanted and go away. Now as demanded, she handed the purse which contained some coins and a few hundred shillings notes to the thug holding her hand.

"Thank you but we want more than this," as if begging for a second glass of water from his host after downing the first one, the gang leader demanded for more money in a cool voice.

"This is enough for sweets and groundnuts. What we want is real money," the team leader commented as an after-thought.

"That's all I have," with a trembling voice Joy answered. This prompted a few slap and kicks here and there to jog her memory.

"Do not beat me again I have remembered," she pleaded raising her hands.

"What have you remembered?"

"There is cash in that basket," and with shaking hands, she dug into the bottom of the basket that held her dirty clothes and retrieved an envelope that held a wad of notes she had intended to bank after the festivities.

After a casual peep into the fat envelope, the thugs hurriedly left, happy with their find. On their way out, the ungrateful ruffians threw a burning match stick on the petrol soaked carpet.

Alone and with no one responding to her cries for help, Joy dragged the burning carpet out through the door they had left open. On her return, she drew a bucket of water from the drum in the corner of her kitchen and doused the flame that was devouring the book shelf. The second bucket went to the curtains behind the shelf whose flames were already working on the ceiling.

After several other trips, the water in the drum was gone but the fire on the ceiling was still raging and rapidly spreading to the rest of the house. She abandoned her fire-fighting mission and daringly dashed into her bedroom. The room was already an oven and with haste, she threw on her bed some of her valuables and a few clothing items. She rolled the lot into a bundle with the bed cover and just as she staggered from the room with her heavy burden the ceiling tumbled down in a ball of fire.

All along, she continued screaming but even the family of her close friend who lived a block away seemed not to hear her cries, or even see her burning house. It was only after running out of the burning house that she saw why; their house was on fire as well and that many other houses in her neighbourhood lit the usually dark estate.

With neighbours busy dealing with their own emergencies, the lone figure of a distraught woman watched as her home went up in smoke. This was barely a day after her business premises in the city center come to a similar ending.

In my reasonableness, (I pride myself as a reasonable girl) I knew that Joy, was still in agony and incapable of answering my question. Like my sister in-law, she sat with her head reclined and could hear her wincing any time the car hit a pothole. Whether the wounds she received from the goons or the loss of her properties hurt most, I could not tell. What I knew was that she had been irritable and useless when it came to small talk.

Unlike my sister who carried all her problems on her face, my mother was different. The turmoil in her mind never showed on her face. In all of my sixteen years habitation in this world filled with some people whose purpose in life is to make your life and mine as hard as possible, I had never seen my mum cry. Not even after the death and burial of my father. She remained calm and even managed to give us the motherly comfort we all needed.

The only exception was an incident that occurred some three weeks after the burial of my father. His grave was still fresh and some of the wreaths we had placed upon it still retained the faded colour of drying flowers. One of his brothers came to visit in the company of some other elders in the family. The meeting had been arranged a few days earlier and proper preparations made to receive the guests. Food and drinks had been served and the table cleared.

I was helping in the service and in my last trip of clearing the table received an innocent request. "Please close the door behind you," my father's brother requested. For a girl who boasted over the substance between her ears, I easily understood that my presence was no longer required.

I closed the door and retreated to the kitchen where Joy was washing the dishes. I informed her that we should keep away from the lounge where serious business was being discussed. If given a choice, I would have liked to participate in the meeting because I felt that my mother was alone against all the visitors.

"What is it that they want?" I had asked my sister.

"I do not know Becky. Maybe it's about the subdivision of the farm,"

"I don't think so. That land was divided long ago. I have even seen the title deed to our land."

I was bothered. Something was terribly wrong and I could not guess what it was. We didn't have long to wait for after a few moments, the peace I had left in the lounge was shattered by an eerie wailing of my mother. We both abandoned the utensils and in alarm dashed to the room.

The visitors and my mother were still seated as I had left them and nothing dramatic seemed to have taken place. However, my mother was weeping with her face buried on her lap.

"What is the matter mum?" I asked with anxiety but the intensity of her weeping could not allow any coherent word in between.

"Mum what have they done to you?" My sister asked in a voice ready to take revenge against the person who had caused my Mum's distress.

"Baba John, why is my mother weeping?" My sister turned to my father's brother.

"Joy, no one has touched your mother. We were just discussing some family business that does not concern you,"

"Anything causing pain to my mother is my personal business with all due respect,"

"In that aspect you are wrong. What we have before us is a matter between your mother and the clan," my father's brother declared.

Joy was about to answer back when my mother tightly grasped her hand, effectively stemming out any answer she was about to shoot. She pulled her into the empty space of the sofa she sat on while motioning me to take the remaining space. For several moments, all was quiet as my mother composed herself.

"Baba John, you are wrong in declaring that my children are not involved in what you wanted to discuss with me," in a calm emotionally charged voice, my mother addressed the visitors. "Whatever decision I make today will affect their lives in a big way," she paused again.

"Children, your father has come to claim us for an inheritance," she dropped a bomb shell.

"What?" Joy asked in astonishment.

"You heard me. That is what he would like but I am

saying a big NO for everyone in this room to hear. I am not available to be inherited and if I ever wish to marry again, I will pick my own man,"

"I assume that you know the implications of you rude rejection. Baba John is trying to fulfill his duties as a brother to your late husband. This is our tradition and it has given warmth and shelter to widows for ages. In your brother in-law, you will have a man to look after you, and your children,"

"I do not need to be looked after. As for the children I trust that with God, all will be well with them,"

"That may be so for now but I would still urge you to reconsider your decision," the spokesman urged as the elders rose and quietly left.

Some six months after that meeting, my mother travelled to our rural home in Siaya on one of her occasional visits. She was surprised to find that our house had been broken into and allocated to one of Baba John's newest wives, while the parcel of land we used to cultivate shared among his other brothers. Though not physically chased away, we had been pushed out of my father's ancestral home. Those were the consequences of my mother's refusal to be inherited. Though she had succeeded in resisting from being inherited as a wife, her brother-in-law had gone ahead and inherited her properties.

When she demanded the restoration of her properties, the elders had ruled that her brother-in-law was acting according to their traditions in taking care of his brother's properties and family. They also ruled that she was free to return home under the care of her brother-in-law. She was informed that traditionally, all the land belonged to the clan and was held in trust by the male members of the clan. In short, a woman had no claim over the properties of her husband.

Chapter Two

I was born at Aga Khan Hospital in Kisumu and when the time came for my going to school, enrolled at MM Shah Primary School which was near our home in Tom Mboya Estate. On completing my primary schooling, I was admitted to Kisumu Girls where I was a day scholar and in form two. The school was due to open in four days' time and like my going back to Kisumu, I doubted whether that was going to happen.

Like many others, I was travelling in the wrong direction. Instead of heading to Kisumu where my school is located, I was travelling in the opposite direction; away from my home, away from my school and friends. We were escaping from a city I called home and in a car that could stall on the road at any moment, a car overloaded beyond imagination, a car whose windscreen was shattered and its body battered with stones.

This made my doubts over my future in Kisumu fair and timely for no person in his or her senses could call such a city home. A city where thugs from the local community looted homes and business premises of the people they considered 'foreigners'. As if looting did not inflict enough pain, they set ablaze what they could not carry away.

That is the city we were escaping from, a city in which a neighbour I have grown knowing, a neighbour who came to 'hold me' when I was born, a neighbour whose children I walked to and from school with almost daily, a neighbour with whom we attended the same church, turned into a vicious blood spilling enemy overnight. I eagerly agreed with one of my teachers who could have said, that such a person who called Kisumu home after such an experience, must have had a head full of *nyuka*. By the way, *nyuka* is porridge in Dholuo.

We were escaping from the tribal clashes that followed the announcement of the disputed presidential election results of 2007. These results led to the great escape after hell broke loose and the rule of law was suspended for a time. Certain communities were targeted and their homes and businesses looted and torched in different parts of Kenya. We, like many other residents of Kisumu and other towns, had stayed holed-up in our house for three days praying that the madness would come to an end.

It never did and in those days, the volume of the T.V. had to be lowered while the children could not play or even cry with the freedom they were used to. In the evenings, the house remained dark and the T.V. provided all the light we needed. We followed the 'breaking news' of what was happening a few meters from our house from both local and international media for all the cameras were focused on Kenya as its citizens destroyed their country. We were hostages in a town that was burning.

I was scared. Everybody was scared.

The children played their games with one eye on the T.V. and the other on the grown-ups and any sudden movement by one person resulted into a scamper for everyone. Gunshots rang from all directions and sounded nearer, and nearer to our house. It was as if the combatants were being pushed towards our house.

We lived in Mountain View Estate in a double storey house and through the window of one of the toilets could see the road that led to the city center. It was busy with the bicycle taxis popularly known as *boda boda* ferrying all types of goods out of the city center. Whether the wares belonged to their customers or not was hard to tell. Those with no means of transport walked and carried their loot in shopping bags like a normal Kisumu resident heading home after a day of nation building.

The real 'protesters' carried their loot in one hand and a machete on the other and would occasionally in swift swings grate them on the tarmac. Their chilling sounds and the imaginations of what a sharpened machete could do brought fear to their purported enemies. Among them was my little nephew.

"What can you see Becky?" Denis, too short to see through the window even upon standing on the toilet bowl wanted to know.

"They are thugs from Obunga," Obunga is a slum not far from the estate we used to live in and a home to many criminals.

"Becky can I have a look please," this was not a plea to create a space for him, but a plea to be lifted to the level of the window, a plea I could not ignore and live in peace, especially under the limited movement out of our compound.

Obligingly, I raised him up and for a few moments watched the continuous flow of people. "Auntie you said the shops were closed," Denis whispered, fearing that the rioters could hear his voice.

"Yes they are my dear,"

"But those people have been shopping," the whispering continued.

"They are not shoppers my dear," I declared as I lowered him. "They are looters,"

"Looters! Who are looters?"

"A looter is a person who takes by force things that they do not own,"

"Oooh. So Angela is a looter as well,"

"Why?

"She looted my car," Denis who was a good learner applied his newest addition in his vocabulary to Angela.

Angela was a girl aged three years and a daughter to our neighbour. A few days ago, she had picked the toy car from our compound and refused to return it claiming that it was hers.

"Angela is not really a looter but a small girl who thinks that all the toys she likes are hers," I had struggled explaining the innocence of Angela in comparison with the actions of the men and women who knew that what they were doing was wrong, but not only went ahead and did it, but did it with a smile. I could see that Denis was not convinced but I had no strength of arguing with a five year boy while dead worried over our safety.

For how long was the child going to be exposed to the on-going violence? Other than that, how long would I personally bear this torture? It was a troubling situation beyond my control and all I wished for was peace; peace to return to my city Kisumu and to the rest of the country. I yearned for the freedom of putting on my best dress and walking with an expectant heart to my church which was just a few meters from our house. I wished for the freedom of going wherever I wished without fear that someone could attack me just because I was not a 'complete Luo'.

I had heard reports of people who had been maimed and others killed; reports of women and young girls who had been raped in different parts of the country just because they could not pass a simple test of speaking in the language of the local community they lived in. There were also many reports of properties that had been looted while others burned down just because their owners came from tribes which were considered foreign.

In my case things were supposed to be different because though my mum was from the Kikuyu tribe, I had a Luo father and name. I also spoke Dholuo fluently. However, I was still in danger from those who knew the ancestry of my mother and I was likely to be a victim just because my 'Luoness' was not complete.

I did not have to go far to know how incomplete I was as a Luo and how foreign my family was, but to the church I was a member of, and to which I attended every Sunday. Our church was a stone's throw away from our house which in a way made it possible for members of my family to attend almost every service with ease. As such, my mum would attend the Morning Glory Service which started at six in the morning daily from Monday to Friday and I would also join her sometimes during the school holiday. She also attended the Wednesday evening prayer meetings every week.

Earlier in the day, we had taken the short walk to our church whose motto was 'Church of Overcomers'. We needed reassurance that despite all the confusion and violence in our country and particularly our city, we would still overcome the evil. I believed that what was happening was the work of the devil and that he would be defeated. I also believed that 'soon and very soon', we would wake up to a morning of peace. I expected to come back with a cheerful heart because I would lay my burdens at the feet of Jesus.

As we prepared ourselves for the service, we could hear the loud singing and knew that we would miss the 'praise and worship session' if we did not leave immediately. This was a favourite part of the service and I used to sing with all my heart. One of my favourite songs during my Sunday school days was just coming to an end as we entered the church compound.

If you are happy and you know clap your hands
(Clap clap)
If you are happy and you know clap your hands
(Clap clap)
If you are happy and you know and you surely want to

As I walked towards the source of the singing, I tapped my Bible against my thighs when we came to the part of the chorus that required the clapping of hands. Likewise, when we came to the part that required the stamping of feet, I added some force to my foot falls and thereby created a feeling of feet stamping in my singing.

During such a time on a normal Sunday, the car park would be full and many worshippers parked by the roadside. That morning it was half empty and even before we entered knew that the church would be half empty as well.

The church compound was always well-kept with the lawns perfectly mowed and the flower beds neat. It was an imposing new building which my family had actively participated in raising funds to construct. It had a wide open foyer and massive wooden doors which were wide open and warmly welcomed the worshippers.

When we entered the church, the singing had stopped and the congregation was settling down, ready to hear the announcements for the week. As predicted, the church was half empty and we had no trouble getting seats in the middle aisle to the left of the pulpit. That was our favourite 'corner' and like many other regular worshippers sat around the same place Sunday after Sunday. In fact our pastor sort of knew where everyone sat regularly and he could with ease pick-out a particular person if the need arose.

As we sat down, I could feel the whole church staring at us. Not that I had turned around and stared back but I had a chill on my back. I shivered a little though it was a sunny morning.

It was as if we were a bridal party walking down the aisle or like the day the president walked into our church without notice. All eyes were on us and we somehow disrupted the service.

Sitting down, I bowed my head with an intention of saying a short private prayer but this was not possible. I could not concentrate and all I could think about was the alarm raising stares we had received. Why did our entrance raise so much interest in a church we attended almost every Sunday of the year? A church which had given us overwhelming support during the burial of my father?

I had so many questions whirling in my mind and after what was like a century of purported private prayers, raised my head and for a moment, looked at my neighbours on my left and on my right. No one was staring at us anymore and all seemed normal other than the emptiness of the church.

"Mum lets go home," I whispered to my mother next to whom I sat.

"Wait a bit," she whispered back. As I waited, the service progressed but I could not follow the preaching. Deep in my heart, I knew that attending church that morning had been a mistake and that even in God's house there were Luos and Kikuyus and that we were all no longer His children. I also realized that many of our friends who were now considered foreigners had skipped church that morning and we were more or less the only 'foreigners' in attendance. In fact it was as if our attendance had defiled the church.

Why had we become undesirables in a church where my late father was once the chairman of the building committee and had contributed heavily to its construction? A church on whose aisle the casket bearing his body had been wheeled? This was the church where my mum was a member of the Women Ministry and actively participated in its affairs. This was the church where I was baptized and attended the youth service and I was even a member of its drama team. This was the church we all loved and innocently thought we would get refuge in times of trouble like this.

This church was our proverbial 'City of Refuge' where everyone was safe, a place where even those who had committed abominable things were received as brothers and sisters.

What crime had we committed? What abomination had we committed? Who had we wronged in the last few days? Personally, I knew that I had done nothing wrong and that if there was a 'crime' I had committed, it was being born to a mother who was a Kikuyu! This implied that my mother who was a hundred percent Kikuyu was in great danger and that like other 'foreigners', she would be hunted down to whatever hole she burrowed in, including this church.

As if holding back the urge to go for a short call, a sat with my legs tightly together as I anxiously waited for my mother to signal that she was ready to leave. This did not happen and after what was like years of waiting, the church service was coming to an end, and the senior pastor arose, raised his hands towards the congregation and said the benediction:

Benediction was to me like the pudding to a meal, or icing on a cake and I must confess that even today, it is one of my favourite parts in a church service. I would at times come late to church but what I could not do was leave before it was pronounced.

The only time I can remember leaving before it was said was on a Sunday when I had trouble with my stomach. I must have eaten something that morning that disastrously disagreed with whatever else was in the tummy and I needed to urgently use the toilet. Like this morning, I suppressed the urge and almost committed a real abomination of defecating in the sanctuary.

I was doing very well until the tail end of the service when the urge to visit the loo came with a new force that I could not withstand. I was sweating as I rose and hurried to the washrooms just before the pastor said the benediction.

Now on this day and for the first time in my life, I doubted the potency of the words of the benediction and wanted to leave before it was said. Actually, its wording made no sense because we had received this same blessing last Sunday but still terrible things I could not imagine had happened.

For instance, during the past week, our restaurant had been looted while the home of my sister had been burned down. Could I still believe that God's face was shining on us? Where was the Lord looking when the thugs were raping women in Manyatta and Nyalenda Estate?

The other looting of the week in Kisumu that shocked my family was that of the house belonging to Rev Wangari Mwai, a senior priest in the ACK church. Rev Mwai and her family were our friends and associated with my parents in many social activities concerning members of the Kikuyu community. There were rumours that some of the looters were members of the church she served. Who would make me understand how the priest who uttered these words of blessing to her congregation would suffer in the same way like a man or a woman who spent his Sunday morning nursing a hangover?

The other bizarre happening of the week was the looting and burning of churches here in Kisumu and in areas around Eldoret. The most chilling was the burning of the Kiambaa church in Eldoret together with the people who had escaped from their homes and sought refuge in the church. The refuge seekers had locked themselves in the church and believed that no one would follow them to this safe haven.

They were wrong.

The thugs had followed them and finding the breaking into the church too involving locked the doors from outside and torched the building. They then stood guard by the windows and slaughtered anyone who tried to escape. Thirty innocent Kenyans who included women and children were killed.

Here in Kisumu I knew of at least two churches which had been looted. One of them was the PCEA Manyatta where the majority of members were Kikuyus. The other one was Abide in Christ Church in Kondele where Rev Muchina, another family friend pastored. This was an iron sheet and timber construction in which members from different tribes worshiped. At the end of the looting, all the furniture and the construction materials were carried away.

Where was the Lord looking when these helpless Kenyans were burned to death? Where was He when His houses were looted and burned down just because they were used and led by foreigners? Where was He when homes belonging to His priests were plundered? If He could not protect His very own houses or people seeking refuge in them, how was He going to protect us from our enemies?

I was leaving the church with many questions but not a single answer, I was leaving church with no confidence of 'facing tomorrow', I was leaving the church hopeless and worried over the future of my family.

"Mum, please skip the hand shaking and let's head home immediately," I hissed at my mother as we exited the church. She had this annoying habit of shaking hands with everyone and chatting with her friends for hours.

She did not respond but did not resist my holding her free hand as I hurriedly steered her out of the church compound. All she could do was acknowledge greetings by waving the other hand that held the Bible. She also maintained her usual smile and friendliness to everyone even at such a time when my heart felt like bursting with loathing to my fellow worshippers that morning. I could not understand how she could still show friendship to a people who had radiated palpable dislike to our presence in the church that morning. How she could do it was a mystery.

We arrived home safely but more worried over our future than before we left for the church. All through the violence in the past week I had felt that all Kikuyus residing in Kisumu were in danger but was yet to personalize the feeling. Those were things that happened to other people, things still far removed from our home. Even the burning of my sister's house and our restaurant was still surreal to me and I was yet to conceptualize it.

The violence continued that day but by around three

in the morning, all was quiet and I assumed that the mobs were in their beds resting their tired bones in readiness for another busy day. Like a rat that sneaks out of its hole at the exit of a cat, my brother drove to the city center with the aim of fueling his car.

"What I have seen is beyond my wildest expectations," he declared on his return.

"What is it you have seen?" I asked with anxiety for I was sleeping in the sitting room and had opened the door for him.

"There was no one on the streets other than the few police officers on patrol. Even the night watchmen who I expected to see huddled in front of their shops were absent. After all, many of the properties they were supposed to be guarding were either burned down or looted and their doors left hanging open. The streets were littered, and plastic paper bags flew around from the breeze from time to time. It's a ghost town in one of Stephen King's novels," Omosh declared.

Of course there was no fuel in all the petrol stations he passed through and he came back feeling trapped.

He was deflated and wondered if the chaos would ever come to an end.

"Would you like to drive with us?" This is the message he found in his mobile phone which he had left in the house. It was from one of our neighbours and ended with a request that he call back.

"We are in the car ready to quit the city. We can drive in a convoy," our neighbour informed him.

He sounded like Lot of the Old Testament gathering his family ready to leave Sodom.

"Its' not possible," he went on and explained of his fruitless search for fuel. Our neighbour assured him that he could drive behind us as we sought fuel on the road to Nairobi.

Could he take the risk? There was no time to debate and within the next ten minutes or so, everyone was awake and ready to go. We threw into a bag what we thought was necessary and departed.

As early as it was, some hooligans were up and busy blocking some parts of the highway with burning tyres. This put on hold any heroic actions like driving over the 'roadblocks'. On each of these 'roadblocks', a wave of a few hundred shillings notes was magical and created a passage for us. A few kilometers out of Kisumu, we found a petrol station which was still operating and we gladly fueled our car.

Of all the 'roadblocks' we had passed through, Sondu Township was the place where I felt the most dreadful danger over our lives. It was around seven in the morning and quite a crowd was hanging at the 'roadblock'. I should explain that Sondu is built in a depression and that on its approach from Kisumu, one has an almost bird's eye view of the shopping center.

Even before we arrived at the 'roadblock', we met two men who were definitely running away from the violence on foot. They warned us of the danger we were driving into and strongly advised us to turn back. We were in a dilemma. In front of us was a mob that was not singing Christmas carols, while the one we had left behind was made up of the *'Bagdad boys'* who had travelled home for the voting exercise!

We drove on.

"Oyawore," one of the boys flagged us down long before we arrived at the 'roadblock' and greeted us in Dholuo.

"Sijambo," my brother foolishly answered in Kiswahili. This was a surprise to him and it was as if all the people who spoke Kiswahili were getting extinct like the El Molo, and that the discovery of a human being

speaking the language became a news item for broadcast to the masses. To him, such a person belonged to the museum for preservation.

"Come on, come on," he shouted with excitement to the hundred plus mob.

"They are speaking in Kiswahili," he explained as he invited them to come over and examine his rare find.

Among the first to arrive was a young man carrying a container with some coloured liquid. He wore a T shirt branded with a portrait of a local MP who had just won the election and the braids of his long hair were held as a pony tail and dangled onto his shoulders.

The one thousand shillings note that Omosh had kept ready to bribe his way through had lost its magic in pacifying the mob which was baying for our blood. However, one of the thugs grabbed the money and run away while quite a number of his comrades pursued him.

Meanwhile we watched in disbelief as the thug with braids hurriedly uncorked the container. Even a fool could tell that he intended to pour the content on our car. Other than the driver's window which was half raised as Omosh pleaded with the mob, all the other windows and doors were locked

In a moment the jerry can carrier splashed some of its contents on the cargo on the carrier and on Omosh whose window was still half open. Everyone was shocked by the smell of petrol that filled the car and even Denis, the boat builder, could tell what was going to happen next.

The thug passed the container to another man and started fumbling with his pockets looking for what we assumed was a box of matches. Just as he succeeded in his search, a girl who in my estimation was of my age pushed forward, grabbed the container which still contained what we now knew was petrol. The man holding it would not let go but the girl was obstinate and continued pulling it away from him. In the process the petrol spilled on all those fighting for the container including the match box holder.

Alarmed that they were wet with petrol, the fighting men let go the container and moved to a safe distance away from the matchbox holder. The girl had the container now, and to the utter shock of the mob, poured some of it on her dress and by holding the can from the bottom, splashed the remainder on those around her, including the man holding the match box.

"Strike that match and we all die with these people," in Dholuo and in a forceful voice she shouted at the match box holder.

The man who now held the match box in one hand and a match stick on the other froze with terror. He looked at his wet clothes and without a word dropped the match stick and at the same time returned the match box to his pocket. Everyone was quiet and watched the girl who in turn stared back at them daring anyone to even raise a finger against us.

"Start the car and drive slowly. Don't worry, I will escort you," the girl ordered. Without a word Omosh started the car and drove through and out of the small town. In her walk besides the car, the girl was joined by five or six other girls who surrounded the car and removed stones and other objects blocking the road.

No one followed us and we drove almost leisurely out of town with the girls on both sides of the car. The mob was left staring at us while chatting in small groups. The girls escorted us until we took the road branching off to Nairobi through Kericho.

Shaking her head, the girl refused to receive the money Omosh offered, "You need that money on your journey than we do. Drive safely," she waved us goodbye. We did not encounter any other hardship and safely arrived at my grandmothers' home in Murang'a in the afternoon.

What I saw that morning will forever remain fresh in my mind and anytime I enter a petrol station, the face of that girl comes into my mind.

Almost immediately on parting with the girls who had saved us, I received a message of encouragement in form of Bible verse from my pastor:

Surely he will save you
from the fowler's snare
and from the deadly pestilence.

These verses taken from Psalm 91 remain my favourite verses especially in times when my heart is troubled. They remind me of Sondu Township and of how the Lord delivered us "with a mighty hand" from our enemies, the day that the Lord commanded "his angels concerning" us.

All the fears and doubts which had been gnawing my heart since the day before when we attended the church service and received hateful stares dissipated. That morning, I experienced God's power in saving, in a way that left me and everyone else in the car sweating and shaking.

People may bring forth clever opinions, equations, interpretation, analysis or any other tool they may use in unpacking situations out of the ordinary. They may even doubt my mental status but to me, that girl was an angel.

This is because I saw with my two eyes a thug almost striking a match to torch our petrol soaked car. I also saw an ordinary girl standing-up against the thug and the mob behind him. What I saw was the saving hand of God. Period! I do not care about what they may think about me. What I simply know, is that God saved us that morning.

What is beyond my understanding is how else a human being, a mere mortal, whether old or young, a believer or not, would interpret such extraordinary happening. Is getting soaked in petrol and almost getting torched an ordinary happening? When did it happen to you last even as you analyze the status of my mind that morning? Do you realize that my death and that of my companions in the car could have happened at the mere striking of that match? Can you explain where this gallant girl got the might of confronting a hundred plus, bhang-smoking mob?

I hope that anyone with a clever interpretation that denies the presence of a great potent hand working behind the scenes in this situation could have been with us in the car that morning! I could have loved to see his or her clever face that morning.

That morning I understood that God has the power to change any situation in our lives. Our homes and businesses may have been looted or even burned down but God was still in control. I realized that God was at work in our fueling the car and in every road block we passed through. I also believed that an angel would be guarding the properties we had left behind.

We may have 'bribed' our way through the many roadblocks we passed through but I realized that God was still at work. I also understood why the 'bribing' could not buy us a passage at Sondu Township, even after offering a whole one thousand shillings note. God wanted to remind us that it was not the money we gave out that gave us a passage but His loving care for us.

The news of our safe arrival at my grandmother's home in Kandara stirred the whole village. There were fears that something sinister could have happened to us as it had happened to many other families. They came in droves bringing all sorts of presents to us. Raw bananas and ripe ones, maize, beans, sugar, tea leaves, milk and even sugar canes were brought. Many could not leave until they heard the whole story of our miraculous escape from Kisumu.

As we enjoyed the warmth of my grandparents' home, shocking news of what was happening in the town we escaped from followed us. Some of the people we knew had been killed while others were injured. Many others were stranded in police stations. Pictures which could have been clips from the Rwandan genocide dominated the headlines as people from different ethnicities retreated to their ancestral homes.

A week after our arrival, we received the sad news that our house in Mountain View Estate was on fire and everything we had left behind had been reduced to ashes. This was not the last bad news we received that week. Within the same week, our farm in Kiboswa where we kept a number of dairy cows that supplied milk to our restaurant was looted. The cruelest thing the looters did was sharing up the animals by cutting them up into pieces even before they were dead. I could not imagine a normal person heaving a leg of a cow on his shoulder while it was still bleeding. The other disturbing news was that all the building materials at the farm were also looted.

I could understand people who looted valuable things from business premises and deserted homes but could not figure out a person who stole building stones. What type of a person could that be? How were the stones transported? On a shoulder? If on the shoulder, how far could the destination of such a person be from the looting site? How long would it take such a person to extract and carry away enough stones to build even a dog's kennel?

In my mind, I came to the conclusion that such a character was most likely a person living not far from the looting site. He or she was also likely a person known to my family. May be he or she was a neighbour we associated with in one way or another. It is also most likely that my parents might have attended a burial or even contributed money for burial in their homes.

With the loss of our Siaya home some years ago, the burning of our house, the loss of our business, and now the looting of our farm, our future in Kisumu looked bleak. We had nothing to go back to and the adults in the family could as well start looking for things to do in Nairobi and Thika.

Chapter Three

We were safe in Kandara but news of the violence, killings, rapes, destruction of properties and general hatred among Kenyans followed us through my grandmother's ancient radio.

Once upon a time, this radio belonged to my grandfather and it was even older than my mother. I was later to know that it was also one of the reasons that my grandfather failed to go abroad like his fellow classmates in Alliance High School. This was because his one dream in life was to one day own a radio which he easily achieved soon after his employment. His other dream was to own a bicycle which he as well achieved and used to cycle to town during his free time.

This radio was also a major source of entertainment to my mum and her siblings when they were young and they would put it on when my grandparents were away and dance to its music.

I could not imagine my mother and her two brothers as young children dancing in those old days long before Kenya gained independence. Even harder to imagine was how our now gnarled grandmother, whose back was bent and who spoke in the slow sort of musical voice, used to be like as a young energetic woman. Her face was now wrinkled and all her teeth gone. The once smooth cheeks were sallow and sunken, while her lips were a thin mass of tough-looking flesh. I also suspected that she tightly held together her lips, like those of a person ready to whistle, in an effort of controlling the now floppy tissues of her face. However, those rather unsightly lips readily produced one of the most charming smiles that I had ever seen.

Uncle Muna and Uncle Mwaniki, the two younger

brothers of my mum, lived with their families in the same compound with my grandmother. They had walked over the moment we arrived and went out of their way in making our stay as comfortable as possible.

They were both taller than my mum and with their balding heads looked like twins. My mum had once told me that they looked like my great grandfather who had died long before I was born.

My two uncles had mobilized their families in providing all the things we immediately needed. They had brought mattresses and other bedding for our use, while Mwaniki had provided a room for Omosh and Daisy. They also cooked and brought over food for our supper.

Going back to the old radio that was part of our family history, my mother had told me that they used to love listening and dancing to music by artists like Fundi Konde and Mwachupa. These were some of the pioneer African musicians. Her other favourite musician was Elvis Presley who in those days dominated the international music scene. He is also referred to as the 'King of Rock and Roll'.

As they enjoyed the music, one thing they were careful about was the length of time they kept it on. This was because dry cell batteries were very expensive and my late grandfather monitored how long they lasted.

If the radio started producing drawn out sounds like those of a person who was drunk long before its schedule, he knew that there had been some unauthorized usage during the month. This would lead to a beating to all the children until they disclosed the wrongdoer.

This radio was basically a rectangular wooden box of about one by two feet with a glass screen of around four inches running on the top of its' face. On this screen was a list of the frequencies from which the radio could receive transmission. Using the biggest dials on the face, one could move a sort of red bar on the screen that worked as the selector of the station that one wanted to listen to. There were other dials which controlled the volume and tone.

In those olden days all that this big lazy radio could receive was two frequencies; one in English and the other in Kiswahili. At scheduled times the broadcast in Kiswahili would give way to other local languages which led to my conclusion that it's big screen and all the listing of all the frequencies it could receive from was extravagant and a waste.

Currently and with all the advancement in broadcasting, all it could receive was the old English and Kiswahili services under a station now known as KBC. We had no access to any of the mushrooming radio stations because they broadcast through FM frequencies which are too modern and complex to the old radio.

We were content with the two radio stations as the source of our news which was in most cases distressing. In fact, we sometimes ignored the radio and in the evening just sat around the fire in the outdoor kitchen chatting while enjoying the company of my grandmother and the quietness of her home. Her home had no hope of ever getting connected to electricity and things like television and the many programs I used to love watching were forgotten.

It is around this radio that almost the entire village gathered to listen to Jomo Kenyatta's speech when this country gained independence in 1963. Using the same magic of its ability to inform, we all gathered around it and listened to news of the dreadful things which were happening in the city we had escaped from, and from the rest of the country.

We also received news through the phone of people who still lived in camps even after some uneasy calm had been restored in the country and people could at least travel safely. Of note were those camped in Kondele Police Station in Kisumu. These were mainly people who were born in Kisumu and had no rural homes to escape to and knew of no other home than Kisumu. They were basically Kikuyus just because of the names they carried.

Among the refugees in Kondele were the family of Nyokabi, a girl we were in the same class at Kisumu Girls and a very close friend of mine. In the past, I had visited her home and even spent the night many times and was familiar with all her family members. In the same way she also used to visit me and at times spend the night with us.

In those days, the days I didn't know that I was different from the people we lived amongst and that I was a foreigner, I took the mastery of Dholuo by members of Nyokabi's family as normal. This was a family where Dholuo was the preferred language in heated arguments. Though bearing Kikuyu names, this family could easily be identified as belonging to the Luo community.

Though there was general tension in Thika, a town near our grandmother's home in Kandara, I had heard of no acts of violence. This was despite the fact that Thika was, and still is, a very cosmopolitan town with both the Kambas and the Kikuyus dominating its population. There are also quite a number of Luo community members living in this town since the days of Tom Mboya who was born in this general area. Another major tribe living in this town is the Kisii who even have an estate going by the name Kisii.

This tension led many families which felt insecure and considered themselves 'foreigners' move to both Makongeni and Thika Police Stations.

I was indignant that such a thing could happen in an area I considered as a safe haven and wanted to reassure the refugees that things will be alright and that it was wrong for anyone to be subjected to such suffering. I wanted to apologize on behalf of all the Kikuyus over their feeling of insecurity which had led them to seek shelter in the police stations. In doing this, I was confirming that I had accepted that I was a Kikuyu and wanted to show them that a real Kikuyu was compassionate and peace loving.

I wanted to show them that a real Kikuyu was civilized and treated all people as brothers and sisters. It was an innocent strange feeling especially in a part of country where hatred against members of other tribes was still very deep. This notion that my new 'people' were not barbarians and respected the sanctity of life was a week or so later shattered when I received the news of violence instigated by the Kikuyus.

Still in my compassionate feelings, I had the opportunity of visiting those camped at Thika Police Station during one of my visits to Thika town with my brother. I found that they spent the night in the police canteen while during the day some went about their normal activities. During my visit, we found children, both boys and girls engrossed in a football game in the small space outside their shelter while some elderly men sat under a tree chatting in low voices. Cooking was going on in the open in another corner of the compound.

We had a bit of extra cash and we had bought loaves of bread and packets of milk which we distributed to the children who had put their game on hold and now gathered around us. Their faces shone with innocence and I wondered what crime they had committed.

Their parents may have voted for whoever they wished but these were children who did not vote and didn't understand what was happening. This saddened me a lot because the injustice done to these children was the same to that which uprooted me from Kisumu.

I was angry with the politicians who spent the day

fomenting hatred among the people and in the evening retreated to their secure leafy homes in Kisumu, Nairobi, Mombasa or any other town and watched Kenyans on Television killing one another. In particular, there was one politician who from time to time held press briefings which always ended with a call for more protests. The day after such a briefing, more violence was witnessed and more precious lives were lost.

The fact that the police warned against such gatherings and usually brutalized the protesters did not deter people from coming out in large numbers. It was as if the people enjoyed those confrontations with the police. What angered me is that many people heeded his calls for protests. I was also equally angered by the excessive force that the police used in dispersing the protesters. Why use live bullets in dispersing protesters. Why couldn't they use tear gas and water cannons? Their brutality fueled the protests.

I was also angry with Kenyans who had or could raise a finger to anyone they considered an enemy. Anyone doing that was a fool who could not see that their enemy number one was not their neigbhbour but the politicians who preached hatred. That neighbour, now considered an enemy, was a mere Kenyan who voted for a presidential candidate of their choice during the polls.

The story of Mama Wambui, a middle aged widow with three children all below ten years and a friend to my sister Joy paints a picture of how life was in some parts of Kisumu during the 2007/8 poll violence. Her family was airlifted to safety after her house and grocery shop was looted.

"Mama Wambui, Mama Wambui," Gabriel, a young man from the Luo community and a grass roots leader in protests against the presidential poll results called, while knocking on the window of her Kiosk.

Mama Wambui lived in a bed sitter which was divided into two parts. In the part that faced the road, she operated a grocery shop and lived in the other part with her children. On a normal day and as late as the time of these urgent knocking, she sold vegetables and fruits which were displayed in a polythene paper roofed structure by the window of her shop. She was a Kikuyu and her rural home was Nyeri.

"Mama Wambui, open, it's Gab, Gabriel and there is nothing to fear," Gabriel had assured Mama Wambui, a woman who knew that this was a lie and that there was every reason to fear for her life and that of her children. She had received reports of plunder, rape and thoughtless destruction of property in many parts of Kisumu and in many other parts of the country. She knew that it was no longer a question of whether, but of when this violence would reach her humble home.

Mama Wambui did not respond but kept still in the darkness of her house. In the last few days, they spent the day holed up in their house and only sneaked out to attend to the call of nature. Cooking was done during the day which removed the need of putting on the lights in the evening. As such, the only light in her house at that time was that of the TV which continually brought distressing news of the raging violence.

"What do you want," Mama Wambui asked in a low voice after a lot of knocking. She had quietly moved to the closed window to the shop.

"I would like some maize meal and cooking oil,"

She pulled out of the shelf the ordered items and put them in a paper bag which she passed over through the slightly opened window. She did not close the window immediately but lingered a little while waiting for the payment.

"And the money," she asked after some uncomfortable waiting.

"I will pay tomorrow, do not worry," Gabriel had for the second time assured. Mama Wambui was getting irritated with these empty assurances from a man who shared nothing else other than a name with Gabriel of the Bible. Gabriel is the angel who delivered the unbelievable and distressing news to Mary that she will become pregnant long before Joseph her fiancée, placed a ring on her finger.

Unlike Virgin Mary who was meeting Angel Gabriel for the first time, Mama Wambui not only lived next to the *miraa* chewing young man whose dirty Mau Mau styled dreadlocks rested on his shoulders, but had in the past given him groceries on credit which he was yet to pay.

It was not only his hair which had a poor relationship with water but the rest of his body which produced a depressing odour, poorly concealed by an equally depressing deodorant that was a close relative to *Binti el Sudan.*

Binti el Sudan is a deodorant that I met for first time at a funeral a long time ago. Those were the ages when the preservation of bodies was a nightmare to the family of the deceased, especially in public hospitals where space in the cold room was limited. You would leave a body properly kept but the attendants would remove it and replace it with another as soon as you stepped out of the mortuary. If no regular monitoring of the preservation of the body was done, one was likely to find it rotten on the day of the burial.

In that funeral, I suspect that such a thing could have happened and the body was in a poor state and needed a strong flagrant to suppress the pungent smell. As such, Binti el Sudan had to be sprayed around the coffin from time to time. After such a generous spray, the container was placed on top of the coffin as if for display. As such, I associate strong nauseating scent with funerals.

"But Gab you still owe me for what you took the other day,"

"I have not forgotten and hope to pay as soon as I

receive my salary,"

"You told me the same thing on the day you took the goods,"

"Don't worry I will pay. On top of that I will make sure that no one bothers you,"

On that dark night and at the height of the tribal violence, she had bolted the window to her kiosk and hoped that Gab would pay for the goods as promised and that he would give protection as promised.

Though Gabriel never paid for the goods he took, or gave protection when a gang descended on her shop and home, he allowed them to hide in his room during the raid and on the following day escorted them to the airport. They spent a night at the airport with other stranded families before they got seats in the overbooked flight.

Violence had erupted in almost every part of the country where people labeled as foreigners had settled. There had been violence in Nairobi, Mombasa, Kisumu, Kitale, Eldoret, Kericho, Nakuru, Naivasha, Meru, Narok and many other parts of the country.

The arrival of displaced people to their home area, whether urban or rural, at times prompted violence. For instance, the arrival of the displaced members of the Kikuyu community in Naivasha prompted violence against members of the Luo community. The scenes were ugly and many innocent Kenyans lost their lives.

One of the most shocking violence on members of the Luo community was that of the family of Bernard Orinda Ndege who lost his entire family of eleven when arsonists torched his home. He escaped with severe burns on his body. Today, his disfigured body especially his face, is a constant reminder of his lost family and of how evil violence is.

* * * * *

The chaos that had engulfed the country was under control and a government of National Unity formed. Mwai Kibaki was to remain the President while the post of Prime Minister was created for Raila Odinga. As long as it brought peace in the country, Kenyans were happy with whoever took the leadership positions.

As for me, getting another school was easy and I got a place in Buchu Girls, a school near my maternal grandparents' home. It was a boarding school and everyone agreed that this school would be good for me.

By the time I went home for my half term holiday, my brother had managed to open a branch of his insurance agency in Thika, and that with time hoped to make it his headquarters. Daisy, who was a teacher, had secured a transfer and they now lived and worked in Thika.

Those yet to get gainful engagement were my mother and my sister Joy. They intended to raise some money for opening a business from the sale of the plots on which our family home had stood and from the farm in Kiboswa.

As a family, everyone was settling down though I missed the kind of life we led in Kisumu. The cold weather was one thing I did not like and I truly missed the warm climate of Kisumu. On top of this, all of my old friends were scattered all over and making new ones was taking longer than I expected. I tried but many of my classmates were reserved and too busy with their studies which to me made no sense. We were only in form three and serious studies for our KCSE examinations were still a long way off.

Despite their serious studies and all the turmoil in my life and that of my family, I easily took the first position in our class which sort of shocked my classmates. I suspect that this also increased their distance from me. They looked at me as a stranger who had no right to score marks better than their own.

My 'sin' of usurping position one in my class could have been easily forgiven and forgotten if I had a name that did not evoke a sense of communal hatred. To my school mates, I was a Luo and Luos were their enemies who had evicted their relatives, or people they knew or heard of, from Nyanza and even from parts of Nairobi.

My name, Rebecca Anyango Otieno, represented all that they hated; a Luo. This was regardless of the fact that my grandparent's home was located just across a river from my new school. All that my new classmates saw was a Luo. This was absurd because I had been rejected and ejected from Kisumu on the basis that I was a Kikuyu masquerading as Luo.

Which tribe did I belong to in a land where survival depended on the tribe you hailed from?

Prior to the ethnic violence, I could have without a thought answered that I was a Kenyan and with no worries continue with whatever I was doing. This changed the moment I felt no longer safe just because I could not prove my 'Luoness'. This was despite the fact that my father was a Luo and I held a Luo name. It was even tougher for my brother Omondi who everyone referred to as Omosh, a corruption of his name that was a very 'Luoish'.

Having been rejected as a Luo and living in a country where one could no longer survive without a tribal identity, I had made myself into a Kikuyu and walked as one. I had even in my actions almost apologized on behalf of all Kikuyus to the refugees at the police station. This was nothing to my classmates and in a controlled school atmosphere where the pupils are supposed to be cultured and above tribal stereotyping, I received all of their anger and hate against the Luos. I was ostracized, isolated, ignored, badmouthed, and all sorts of actions that in a passive way shouted rejection were applied against me.

I would join a group of girls chatting and one by

one, they would all melt away and leave me standing alone. There were other incidences where I was denied a seat on certain tables in the dining hall on the guise that the seat was reserved for someone who was yet to arrive. At other times I would pass by a group of girls and they would break into a loud laughter directed at me. These uncomfortable incidences were a torture but I tried as much as possible to control my temper. I therefore took refuge in my studies and avoided gatherings which were entirely social.

What was hard for me to understand was why everyone ignored the fact that my mother was a Kikuyu whose home was not very far from the school. To be discriminated against in Kisumu and also in Murang'a was distressing and showed how deeply rooted tribalism was.

While still in Kisumu, I saw one of my cousins who lived in Europe in the same dilemma. Her father is a German while his mother is a Luo. While in Germany she is seen as black girl and in Kenya as *mzungu*, a European which made her very uncomfortable.

Back to my new school this situation was to change after one of my school mates fell sick and was hospitalized. Wacuka was her name and she was a form four student whose slenderness accentuated her height.

Until her illness, I looked at Wacuka as someone who had control over her weight and needed not worry what she ate. This was a real issue to me because I was over-weight despite my routine exercising and at times rigid dieting. I could have given anything to attain Wacuka's slimness until I knew that she was a very sick girl who was always on medication. I later gathered through *mucene* (gossip) that she suffered from a chronic disease and that she had been hospitalized several times in the past.

She was a girl easy to notice but we had never

interacted on a personal level. What I could remember was that she had been part of a group of girls who had jeered at me when I walked past where they stood in one of the corridors. How active she was in this I can't tell, but what I know for sure is that she had not shielded me against the harassment.

The Head Teacher had announced that she was hospitalized and needed prayers, and like a good Christian I prayed for her every night before I slept. Her situation worsened and a few days later received an urgent plea for blood donations. Blood donors were many but what she needed was specific; blood group O negative. People with this blood group are commonly referred to as universal blood donors. They can donate blood to anyone but they can only receive blood from their fellow O negative blood group donors.

For Wacuka, three donors were identified but what they gave was not enough, and much more was needed.

I had joined the school the term before and no one knew the blood group I belonged to. On top of this, I was to my school mates a Luo and I had a feeling that blood from a Luo could not mix well with that of a Kikuyu! Apart from that, I was under no obligation to donate blood to a Kikuyu, more so to a Kikuyu girl who not only hated me, but had been one of my tormentors.

A few days earlier, the three girls had done their donation but more blood was required. More pleas for donors were made and though not asleep like Jonah of the Bible, I heard the pleas but kept silent. All around me everyone was worried over what might happen to Wacuka but my heart was as hard as a stone. I even justified her sickness as a punishment for some sins she had committed including jeering at me.

That night, the night of the second plea, I dreamt that I was travelling to Takawiri Island in Lake Victoria on a geographical tour with some of my old school mates of Kisumu Girls in a boat christened Nineveh. The name was boldly written on its sides and long before I even knew that it was the boat we were to use wondered why anyone would give such a sinister name to a vessel. The name was so ominous that it brought to mind the image of a capsizing boat. My fears were not baseless because marine accidents in the lake were common.

Strangely, among my fellow travellers was Wacuka. Not the ailing Wacuka but a jovial sailor who was laughing and singing like everyone else. I was also not the sulking and the detached Rebecca I had become, but a girl who was cheerful and happy with life.

The boat was actually a canoe which was 30ft long and powered by a motor engine. Along its body, a bench had been built and passengers sat facing one another with the space in between used for luggage. We had been instructed that each of us was to remain seated and avoid sudden movements all through the journey.

After sailing for some time, the waters became very rough with a strong wind buffeting us away from our destination. I could not see any land or vessel around us and all around was the stormy waters. Like everyone else, I feared that there would be no one to rescue us in case the boat capsized, and that we would be lost with no trace like the Malaysian airplane which plunged into the ocean and has never been found.

The boat was still rocking and riding waves taller than it was in height and we saw death staring at us. We were wet from the splashing water while what we could not block or soak with our bodies worryingly gathered on the floor of the boat. From our awkward sitting positions, we tried scooping it out with every conceivable container with little success. What was left of our joyful singing a moment ago was a horrifying scene of wet-frightened girls miserably trying to save a sinking boat.

In the last part of the dream, I was no longer a school girl but Jonah, the fellow who defied God and refused to take a ship that could have taken him to Nineveh on a preaching mission. My fellow travellers had found me sleeping while they frantically tried to save the boat. They also found out that I belonged to a blood group that could save the ailing Wacuka but I refused to donate. This was the reason God was angry with us and wanted to finish all of us by drowning.

My fellow travellers were no longer singing and jolly but hostile members of my new school who wanted to save themselves, by tossing me into the raging water. I resisted and I was fighting back with all of my might while shouting my reasons for keeping silent. This is the moment I woke up, shaken and drenched in sweat.

As I recovered from the shock, I got out of the bed and like a sleepwalker headed to the room that our matron spent the night.

"Mrs Muturi, Mrs Muturi," I urgently called while knocking on the door.

"What is it," she asked with anxiety as she opened the door.

"I would like to give Wacuka blood,"

"At this time?"

"Right now if it can be arranged," she did not waste time and immediately called the school driver and by eight in the morning I was waiting for the door to the blood bank at Thika District Hospital to be opened.

By ten O'clock tea break, I had donated blood, seen the still weak Wacuka and was back in school. What I could not take was the tea for I had been treated to a heavy breakfast of bacon and sausages at Fourteen Falls Lodge in Thika.

Chapter Four

With no friends to relate with or a TV to watch, I spent most of my time with my grandmother when school was closed for the April holidays. She was caring and loving and with her limited resources made our lives as comfortable as possible. In her free time or as we worked, she had stories and stories to tell and it appeared that she longed for a listener.

In me, she got a keen listener who wanted to know the history of our family and what life was like in the days when my parents were young. I also wanted to know why my mother had chosen to be married to a Luo, while she could have easily settled for a man from her community. If I understood the history of my parents, I would then know better who I was.

What I knew was that my parents had met in Thogoto Teachers College and married soon after their graduation. The young family had then moved to Kisumu where they had taught and raised a family. I knew that we had two sets of grandparents; one in Seme in Siaya where my father was born and the other in Kandara in Murang'a District. When my father was still alive, we used to spend parts of our school holidays in Seme near Kisumu, and at least once a year travelled to Kandara.

I remember my times in Seme with sadness for this is where I enjoyed the best of my time during the school holidays. Together with other children in the family, we helped in grazing the many cows and goats that my grandmother owned and while doing it played all sorts of games. After the day's work, we would all dash to the lake and plunge into the cool water. As a visiting child from the city, my grandmother spoiled me with all sorts of local delicacies that I would travel back to Kisumu already planning for the next visit.

I am the last born in a family of five, two boys and three girls. Joy is the eldest followed by Tom, a brother I know from a photograph taken while still a toddler. He died before his third birthday from a severe bout of malaria. Omosh, born in 1966, is the third born while Petronila, the girl I follow, in 1970. I was born twenty years later which made many people confuse Petronila as being my mother and my mother, as my grandmother. This did not bother my sister and there were many times she bothered not with explanations, especially in the absence of my mother. She accepted the honour of motherhood and I think she used to enjoy it.

She did not have long to wait for motherhood proper, for in my second birthday she got her first born daughter, Leah. Leah was born in our home and we were brought up together. It was while in class three that I came to know that she was actually not my sister but my niece.

Nobody ever mentioned Leah's father until six years ago when he appeared from nowhere and like a long forgotten left luggage, claimed my sister and her daughter. I was devastated for this claim not only destroyed the structure of my family as I knew it, but also took away my best friend.

"Why don't you refuse to go," I had quietly incited Leah.

"You know I would, but I do not want to cause pain to mum. I will be coming over for visits over the holidays. After all you are soon joining a boarding school and you will be away from me most of the time."

Objection to this union also came from my mother who cautioned Petronila on the wisdom of moving in with a man who had abandoned her when she needed him most.

"Mum, I have always loved this man and I feel that he is the only one for me," my sister had pleaded with mother.

"I'm just raising the red flag but the decision is entirely yours. However, he has to do things properly for him to get you. But always remember that this home is the only home Leah knows and I reluctantly allow you to take her away," my mother cautioned.

Doing things properly entailed the payment of the dowry and a church wedding for my sister. Mugambi, for that is the name of the stranger claiming my most favourite sister and niece, was a man from Meru. He came prepared and within six months, all the conditions that had been laid out were met and in a colourful wedding held at St. Stephen Cathedral in Kisumu, my sister was given a warm send-off.

The year that my sister married was a sad one for me. I was almost settling down to a life without my niece when the news of the sudden death of my grandmother from Seme came. I was in shock for days and mechanically went through the burial rites. A week later, we laid her to rest next to my grandfather who died before I was born.

Just when I thought that I was used to a life without Leah and my grandmother, another tragedy hit my family. This was far greater than I could bear. My father who was a retired teacher had travelled to Nairobi on some business. On his way back, the bus they were in collided with a trailer at Salgaa, a few kilometers from Nakuru. My father was among those who died.

To say that I was devastated would be the misstatement of this century. I don't think that I can illustrate my feelings on receiving the news. I loved my father in a way no one can understand. Not even my mother. I do not imply that others in the family did not love him, or that I did not love my mother as deeply. That is not the case. My wish is to express my deep feelings for my father.

When still a young girl, I could not go to bed until he came from wherever he had gone. When he knew that he would be coming late, he would take the trouble and inform me before he left in the morning, or call later with the information.

In the evening he would assist with my homework, or we would watch my favourite programs on TV. He dropped and picked me from school whenever he was available and there was nothing I could not tell him. He was my best friend. That is the father whose sudden departure I was informed of. Would I believe it? No Sir. No Madam, I couldn't. They must have made a mistake. Such a person could not die like that.

Two weeks after the arrival of the dreadful news, we buried him in a ceremony attended by thousands. Having been a teacher for over thirty five years, there were many old students who came to say goodbye to *japwonj*. I went through the motions of the ceremony like a zombie while clinging to my mother's hand.

It took years for me to accept that my father was no more. Even today, any single achievement I make causes my mind to flash to my father. How he could have been joyful over my good performance in my class eight exams!

The death of my grandmother, followed by that of my father and the fight over properties severed my connection with the remaining family in Seme in a sad way. Other than the graves of the two loved ones, I had nothing left to pull me for a visit. This may have created the closeness I felt for the only remaining grandparent in Kandara and the need of knowing the family background. What I knew of the family branch in Seme was also sketchy but I hoped to fill in the gaps in the future.

With no TV to take the center space in our evenings, I would sit with my mother Wanjiku, and Julia, my proper shosh around the fire while preparing supper and in segments, stories of the olden days of the two women came out. In that semi-darkness of her smoky kitchen, I would feel pains that the two women went through as young girls and at other times enjoy their good times.

The atmosphere of our new home brought calm and patience in my mother that I had never seen. She could sit for hours and tell me stories she had never told me before. For the first time in my life I saw her free from the long hours that the hotel business in Kisumu demanded. She woke up and went to bed as she wished with no worries over the attention demanding business. It was as if she was on a long holiday.

Sitting under a mango tree whose history was as old as that of our family my mother narrated a story that transported me back to the days before Kenya gained independence. It was an incredible story of pain, blood and sweat punctuated by love.

Chapter Five

"Your grandfather was the strongest person I had ever known, the most handsome and loving man that ever walked this planet. This is the person I used to run to when the bullies in our estate exercised their might on me, or when I got a thorn into my tender feet," my mother made the opening statement in a story that made her voice tremble with emotion.

"With authority that left them shaking, he would reprimand the bully and promise a beating that had never been heard of, if the annoying bully ever pointed a finger at me again. As for the thorn, he would with soothing words almost painlessly remove it," my mother Wanjiku, simply known as Ciku in those days, continued.

"*Guka*, do you know what they did to my father?" My mother, then a small girl had asked her grandfather soon after their arrival from Naivasha. I knew that my parents had once lived in Naivasha but I had never known the reason they moved out.

"I do not know Ciku. Please tell me," her Guka had encouraged.

"Imagine they handcuffed him like a thief, and lifted him like this. They were strong men and his toes hardly touched the ground," my mother had illustrated how her father was arrested by holding behind the shorts that Muna, her younger brother, was wearing.

Though not as strong as those men, she almost raised him from the ground and forced him to walk with his toes hardly touching the ground. It was a funny sight and Jecinta her cousin laughed in a high pitched voice.

"What is so funny," looking at Jecinta, she had demanded in a voice heavy with anger. The arrest of her father was not a laughing matter and anybody who laughed over it could never be her friend again.

Had the laughter come from somebody else, maybe her reaction could have been different. But coming from her cousin, it all sounded hostile and eerie and reminded her of the dislike she had shown them since the day they arrived at her grandparents' home from Naivasha.

"Leave me alone, you are hurting me," Muna who was still hanging halfway in the air from the back of his shorts protested.

"That is enough Ciku. I have seen and understood the brutal force they used on your father. And you little rascal, like Ciku has told you, there is nothing funny in the arrest of your uncle," her grandfather had reprimanded the annoying cousin.

"And tell me, did your father resist arrest?" Her grandfather asked once again turning his attention to Ciku.

"Not at all *Guka*, those men were just mean and wanted to humiliate him,"

She was aged ten and the first born in a family of three. Her younger brother Muna was nine while Mwaniki, the youngest in the family was barely four. Small bodied and appearing younger for her age, many people doubted that she was as old as she claimed when the question of her age arose.

"Until our forced travel, I was a class four pupil at Mwariki Intermediate Primary School in Naivasha. That year, I could have sat for examinations. Those exams were crucial in that they were to be used in selecting those to be promoted to class five in the following year," she paused for a moment.

"Failure to sit, or worse still, a poor performance, could have forced me to repeat my class four, a situation I could not even imagine. It could have been a disaster if I was forced to repeat class four because Muna, (or at least his classmates) who was currently in class three, would have caught up with me. This was not healthy for my self-esteem and authority both in school and home. It could have been a torment and I could have done anything to avoid it," my Mum continued with her narration.

Worried as she was, she clearly understood that her fate was sealed and not only was she going to miss her promotion, but there was a likelihood that her schooling had come to an end. This was a grave situation for the end of her education meant the death of her dreams of one day becoming a teacher. However this was not as worrying as the fate of her parents. What had happened to them? Would she ever see them again? Those were questions that kept the small girl awake and were made worse by the daily cry of her baby brother calling for her mother. Would her delicate family survive the absence of her parents?

For a girl of her age and the current head of her broken family, crying in front of her brothers was a thing she could not do. It could have shattered their trust as she assured them that everything would be alright and that their parents would be coming home soon. Frustrated and tormented as she was, she had to keep her emotions and tears under control.

Every time she looked at their sad faces, tears would cloud her eyes but she always fought them back. Thus every night, when everyone fell asleep, Ciku would do her weeping. In the morning, she would rise tired but ready to go to school only to realize that there was no school and no mother to prepare her breakfast. She would slump back to bed she shared with her cousin and wait for her hosts to rise.

To her annoyance, Jecinta would continue sleeping and snoring as if she was on holiday. "Wake up, wake up," she would nudge her until she got out of bed. This she did daily and could not understand how a person could go to school late every day. For the next hour or so, she would lay back and think of her future and that of her two brothers who were still sleeping. She would think of her parents wherever they were and pray that God would keep them safe until they were reunited.

Going late to school every morning was not the only cause of the strain between my mum and her cousin. Its cause was not even her uncontrolled laughter over the arrest of her father. It went back to the day they arrived in this new home. Jecinta had looked at the three tired and dirty-manure-smelling children like a dead rat brought into the house by a cat. Under the watchful eye of her grandfather, she had dutifully given them a limp handshake.

"That is the voice of Joy," my mother interrupted her narration. Joy and my grandmother had gone to the market to buy some provisions we needed. "I think we will continue in the evening."

That evening, as we took our dinner, I reminded her that she had a story she had to continue telling.

"What story," my sister Joy wanted to know.

"Of her childhood,"

"I would like to hear it as well,"

"All you have to do is to listen," my mum invited. Like in an auto gear, my mother went on to give a narration which I hoped to put down together as a book in the future. We had taken our dinner and each of us held a cup of tea which we sipped from time to time.

"Our problems as a family started with an urgent knock on our door. *Ko ko ko*, the urgent knock vibrated in our one roomed house. *Ko ko ko* open the door, whoever was knocking ordered in an authoritative voice," my mother started her narration without further prompting.

"Who is it?" My father shouted for the benefit of the person knocking.

"The police,"

"Wait a moment then,"

"*Ko ko ko*, open up this very moment or we break the door," the impatient knocker continued even before the moment my father had asked for was over.

"As the communication with the men outside our door continued, my father dressed quickly while whispering some instructions to my mother. We were all awake and shaking with fear over what the police wanted in our house this early in the morning."

My mother went on to narrate how her father eventually opened the door and in a moment they were all ordered out of the house at gunpoint. "It looked foolish pointing a gun at my father, a man who was law abiding and a respected employee of Kenya Uganda Railway. I realized that their foolishness went deeper than I thought when the same guns were directed at my mother and us,"

"The squad raiding our home was made up of five African policemen locally referred to as *ngati* (home guards) under the leadership of a white police officer, popularly known as a *johnnie*,"

They claimed that there were guns and other equipment in the house which the Mau Mau used in terrorizing the Europeans. This was absurd and nothing could have been farther from the truth.

"If that is what they are looking for, then my father will be safe", Ciku innocently told herself.

"I had never seen a gun at close quarters other than the ones that were pointed at us, and in fact, if they had bothered asking me, I could have told them the truth and saved them the trouble of conducting a search,"

In a few moments the house which was always neatly arranged and clean was in a total mess. Mattresses, bedding, clothes, utensils and other odd items littered the floor which was wet with porridge.

Earlier on, the impatient *ngati* had kicked the gourd that always contained sour porridge and was kept in one corner, and smashed it. This was not an accident but an investigative action by a force too dignified to pour the contents of the gourd in order to find out whether bullets were hidden there or not. It was a very shameful act that showed disrespect to the people they claimed to govern.

The results were a broken gourd, spilled porridge (and the mess it entailed) but no bullets. They had turned the one roomed house upside down but no guns or anything incriminating was found. Frustrated, they ordered her father to accompany them to the police station to answer a few questions (the police even today do not have many questions for the person being arrested. They always take the prisoner away to answer a few questions!).

"I do not think that Muna and Mwaniki really understood what was going on, other than that the policemen were taking our father away and that they had to do everything to save him," with a faraway look my mum continued.

"All through, we were all calm and quiet as we watched the futile search. Things 'became elephant' when they handcuffed my father and pushed him towards their Land Rover. We started wailing and my mother who was heavy with another baby could do nothing other than hush us down and gather us around herself,"

"Muna was the most difficult to control," my Mum continued with the long narration. "He had learned at a tender age that he was the man of the house when my father was away. This responsibility became even more crucial when that father he was to act for was being taken away. He was not like our leaders today who will privately pray for, or even arrange the elimination of the person under whom they work for them to occupy his or her vacant post. He was a true patriot and did everything within his might in protecting him. Currently, he held onto his father's trouser as they made him walk on his toes towards the black Land Rover,"

"Ambia toto nyamaza ama mimi chapa wao sana," the white policeman shouted. Roughly translated the man was telling my mother in broken Swahili that she should hush the children down and if not, he would beat them up thoroughly. This is a threat he fulfilled a few moments later. He cut a stick from a nearby bush and as promised, thoroughly thrashed Muna who had taken his rescue mission all the way to the Land Rover,"

"Leave my son alone! Leave him alone," her father in anguish but helpless, shouted at the policeman in English. Ignoring him, the white man delivered more thrashes to the boy before jumping into his seat beside the driver. A kick on the chest by a *ngati* who was already in the back of the Land Rover left Muna in pain and sprawled on the dusty floor weeping. Before he could rise up again, the Land Rover dashed off.

"That boy is a Mau Mau already," the white man breathlessly declared as he locked his door.

"That is true boss. It is the father who is training him," the African driver eagerly agreed. Training a child to be a Mau Mau was a criminal offence that could send a man to detention for a long time. In a cloud of dust, the Land Rover left the compound headed to the police station which was some two kilometers away.

"All through this commotion, one would have been excused in imagining that we didn't have even one neighbour who could have come to our rescue. We had neighbours. Not one but many for we lived in a housing block that was made up of ten one roomed units. A similar block faced ours across the dusty courtyard. This early in the morning, the courtyard was usually busy with some women fanning their jikos, while others hung their washing on the lines which crisscrossed the compound. Later in the day, tens of children would gather here as they played their games," my mum paused as she took a sip of her tea.

"That morning, the arrival of the police had put a stop to all these activities. It was as if the estate was uninhabited. Through the cracks of the almost closed doors, the families watched the unfolding drama with fear," my mother painted the atmosphere of their old estate that morning.

It is easy to understand the behavior of their neighbours for what was happening that day was a common occurrence. Many had suffered the same treatment in one way or another. Children who still had their father with them knew that the same predicament that had befallen their playmates could happen at any time. Meanwhile, they did what was expected; running and burying themselves in their one roomed houses.

Even witnessing such an arrest was a crime under the many ambiguous emergency rules. Rules that could be bent to suit the situation and wishes of the white man, rules through which they thought they would castrate the minds of the natives turning them into zombies, a people that did the bidding of their colonial masters.

"If the white man ever made a mistake in his fight against the Mau Mau, the biggest one was the manner in which they arrested my father that morning. Something bitter like bile was poured into my heart creating a fury I could not control," my mother confessed. "When I grow up, I will pay the '*wabeberu* back for what they did to my father," she had sworn that morning.

'*Wabeberu*' was the name they used in reference to the white colonial masters. The word was fashioned out of the Kiswahili word '*beberu*', the he goat. A he goat is known for its harassment to the she goats in its ceaseless quest for a mating partner. Thus, the colonialists were *'beberus'* in the way they continually bothered the natives.

To a white man the word 'native' acquired a new meaning when applied to an African. It meant a people who were so backwards and primitive that crude force was to be used in educating them in the ways of the modern culture and religion. By force, the European culture had to be hammered into their primitive minds. This education took all spheres of life.

"What the white man did that morning was to create a new breed of Mau Mau's. There was no reason to arrest my father in such a brutal manner, neither had my brother committed any crime to warrant the beating he received. My brother was a bit of a nuisance, I agree, but that could not earn a child of that age a kick on the chest from an adult in military boots commonly known as *kafunja ndua*. My heart was full of hate and to date, whenever I see a white man, my mind goes to that morning,"

"What is *kafunja ndua*? I interrupted the narration.

"The colonialist made the making of our local brew *muratina* illegal and the police would search the village for illegal brewers. If they found the brew which was usually kept in a big gourd called *ndua*, they would kick the container with their military boots and crash its belly and the brew would spew out. That is how the military boots came to be known as *kafunja ndua*," my mother explained.

"As young as I was, my interest in this Mau Mau thing that was giving the white man sleepless nights was heightened. I had heard of Dedan Kimathi, Mathenge, General China, Matenjagwo and other freedom fighters before, and never took keen interest. Things changed. I wanted to join them as soon as I was old enough. The problem was that I had never heard of a woman who was a Mau Mau. Would they accept me? I didn't know and needed to know. A good source of this information was my grandfather and soon after our forced move to his home, sought answers though indirectly,"

"But *Guka* are you a Mau Mau," she had asked her grandfather.

"My child every person who is not happy with what the white man is doing to our people is a Mau Mau. If I were young, you could not have found me watching helplessly at what is happening. I could have joined the fighters in the forest. But now I am an old man and cannot live for long in the cold forest," the old man had explained.

"But *Guka* you told us that you were born before the white men came to our land," Ciku, my mother took him back in time.

"Yes,"

"Why did you allow them to settle down? You could have simply kicked out the very first white man who showed up," my mum reasoned.

"That is a valid argument my daughter. As a nation we are reaping the fruits of our mistakes. On the other hand, the coming of the white brought some advantages which we could never have experienced had we locked them out,"

"What are those advantages?"

"Some of their medicines are superior to ours, and diseases like cholera which used to wipe-out entire villages have been put under control,"

"Then you should have put a control to their activities," she suggested.

"It was a complicated matter and one thing led to the other. The first batch to arrive appeared innocent with their funny looks and beliefs and we saw no harm in hosting them. We even allowed some of our people to join them with a hope of knowing them better. Little did we know that they would be corrupted and turned against us,"

"That was not very wise,"

"I agree with you my daughter. They appeared foolish in their religion. It was like allowing a child to play with its toys. Why bother with a people who sounded confused in their own beliefs? For example, they told us that Christianity was the only 'true religion' and that our age old God, locally known as *Ngai* was a fake. They termed His residence at the top of Mt. Kirinyaga as a mere rock covered with snow. The most awkward thing about their new religion was that as sophisticated as they were, they could not get a local name for their God! What did they do? They called him *Ngai*, the name of the God the backwards natives worshiped! What about His holy place on Mt. Kirinyaga? They built a church and declared that that was His holy residence."

My mum's grandfather told her that there were many brave women who were fighting side by side with Dedan Kimathi in the forest. A good example was Field Marshal Muthoni Kirima. This Mau Mau heroine was their neighbour and had followed her husband into Nyandarua forest and made very notable contribution in the struggle for independence.

"After the sounds of the Land Rover faded away, the doors to our neighbour's houses started opening. Not that they opened as one would for a long lost friend who had paid a surprise visit. No. That could have been too risky and could have made such a person appear like a sympathizer to the Mau Mau. Thus, the doors opened slowly with people peering for a possibility of one of the guards lingering behind,"

"Mama Ciku," a neighbour and colleague to my father called.

"Come in Baba Akinyi," my mother welcomed him. Akinyi was his daughter, a girl slightly younger than I was and one of my friends in the estate. We also attended the same school.

"Wa wa wai!" Baba Akinyi exclaimed in astonishment on seeing the chaos in our house. "What was the use of all this? What were they looking for?"

"Guns,"

"Guns? Even if your husband was a Mau Mau would he be that foolish to keep such things where his children sleep?" All this time he stood at the door post while they put the room to its old form.

"It is okay but our God from his high seat of Mt. Kirinyaga sees all. We are like a poor baby gazelle that helplessly watches its mother being eaten by a lion. But this madness will soon come to an end," in a sad voice her mother had predicted the end of the white rule.

"Other neighbours came and expressed their sympathy over the arrest of our father but none had the courage of following the Land Rover to bail him out. Not that we blamed them or expected them to make such a visit. They couldn't. For anybody doing that was as well branded a Mau Mau and thrown in jail together with the person he or she had gone to rescue. Thus one by one, the neighbours went back to their day's activities,"

"The house was back in order and she cooked some porridge which we always took for breakfast. This porridge was different from the sour one kept in a gourd that had been broken by the naughty *ngati*. It could be made from sorghum, millet or any other cereal my mum fancied. We took it in calabashes and no sugar was added. In those days sugar was a luxury that only the rich could afford. It is not that this bothered us one bit. It never did. After all, we had never tasted porridge with sugar before,"

"Sugar and tea wise, the only exception was your grandmother," she pointed a lazy finger to my grandmother Julia who had a cup of tea in her hand. She nodded in agreement with her daughter. "She took her share of porridge but always 'chased' it down with a cup of tea. She claimed that she suffered a headache if she missed her tea. How true this was I can't tell but your grandmother is not a person to lie over a cup of tea, especially a cup of tea she had the choice of brewing or not," she paused and looked at my grandmother who gave her an encouraging toothless smile.

"She always told us that lying was a waste of time for the truth would be known with time. This was true especially when we tried to lie to her. She had a way of detecting a lie. In those days digging for the truth from any of us was easy for the sight of her cane had the magic of loosening the tongue for the truth to freely flow. That reminds me that I should get another cup of tea. I think there is a little remaining in the flask," she requested and for the next few moments I was busy serving tea.

"She could see and recognize a lie from miles away," she continued as if we had not stopped her narration on my handing over the tea. I looked at grandmother's wrinkled face and had trouble imagining her as a young woman disciplining her children. I had always known her as old and easy going.

Chapter Six

"Going back to the happenings of that morning, we took our porridge and I chased mine with a cup of tea as your mother has said," Julia, my grandmother took over the narration from my mother, Wanjiku aka Ciku.

"I instructed your mother to wash the dishes and look after her brothers while I visited the police station to find out how your grandfather was faring." Julia continued the narration while looking at me.

Though others feared the risk of such a visit, a spouse to the prisoner was treated differently. However, the visit was a waste of time for other than the confirmation that her husband was held there, she was not even allowed to see him. She was to hear details of his suffering four years later from Mwariama, their neighbour. He had visited their home as soon as he arrived from Manyani where he had been detained with my grandfather. He told Julia that her husband had died of cholera which had swept hundreds in the concentration camp. Together with tens who died every day, he was buried in a communal grave dug and filled by a bulldozer.

Each morning, the dead were piled on the shovel of the bulldozer which transported the bodies and like garbage dumped them in the trench.

"On arrival at the police station, your grandfather (May the Lord rest his soul in eternal peace) was put in a cell which was already too small for the number of prisoners it held. Many were detained for offences which in one way or another touched on the Mau Mau movement," my grandmother continued with her narration.

One of them, an old man who worked as a housekeeper in a nearby ranch, was accused of stealing some money from his employer. This crime which could have led to a trial and a possible jail term was viewed differently under the emergency rules. He was accused of theft with an aim of assisting the Mau Mau with the proceeds. This earned him a direct ticket to the concentration camp.

Another prisoner was accused of being drunk and uttering words which incited people against colonial rule. In a sober society the inciting words he was accused of uttering were the ordinary ranting of drunkards on their way home. Like his comrade the thief and many others who faced similar flimsy accusations, he waited for transport to the dreaded concentration camps without trial.

Prisoners were transported on a weekly basis as the colonial government was too busy arresting that they forgot the existence of the court of law. Not that much justice could have been received under the emergency rules.

"Rucacu mtu wa reli (the railway man),"

It was the turn for my grandfather to be interrogated. There was no other Rucacu, nor any other person working with the railways for that matter in that cell. He had been sitting right behind the closed door of the crowded cell and when the door opened, he literally sat under the nose of the guard summoning him. There were three guards crowding the door, all of them Africans and members of the Kenyan Regiment. One of them crammed a pair of handcuffs on his hands, while another one closed the door to the cell.

"Sandwiched between the two guards, and another one holding him from the back of his trousers in their trademark fashion, they led him to one of the offices. All the hassle while moving him within the police station was of no use because every corner they turned armed policemen stood guard. It was a sight that could have discouraged anybody with an idea of running away,"

"He was made to stop in front of one of the offices

whose door was closed. In a hand writing too big to fit in one line on the face of the door, the name of the officer who sat behind it was written; "Raymond Trafford Jr, Chief Inspector of KR."

As if a simple knock could have torn apart the heavy wooden door, one of the guards tapped lightly and waited. After what appeared as ages (especially when anxious to face the man who held your fate) the guard knocked again.

"Come in," Raymond, the man who held my grandfather's fate shouted from behind the closed door.

The guard eased the door open to an office dominated by a desk that was way too big for the space. Behind it the Chief Inspector, a man too young for the post sat. He was a disappointment to my grandfather who had expected to find an older man sitting behind the desk. The man facing him was in his early twenties, and his title sounded too grand for him. He was a tall thin young man, who wore clothes that must have been borrowed or even discarded by a person much bigger in size. The previous owner was probably his father who had grown too heavy for the clothes. They hung on him like a scarecrow erected in a garden.

"What the young man lacked in age and stature was compensated by his deep hate for the black people," Julia my grandmother continued with her narration.

"His hate was not limited to the Mau Mau he had vowed to hunt to the last drop of his blood, but also to his fellow African KR officers. This hate turned into a cruelty that was yet to be shown by any other officer while screening a prisoner. Screening was an exercise that men, women and even children went through under the emergency rules. They were interrogated over their association with the Mau Mau until they confessed. If a confession was not forthcoming, the prisoner was locked up in remand where torture and questioning continued,"

During the screening, Raymond would sit in one

corner of the room and give direction at every stage of the interrogation. Not that he would touch the prisoners in extracting a forced confession. No, he was too superior to soil his hands by touching the dirty Africans. By a flick of his fingers he had become an expert in breaking down hardcore Mau Maus, sworn to an oath of silence.

His grandfather was among the Boers in a caravan that was headed to the areas beyond the Rift Valley, later to be called the white highlands. Sick and tired from the long journey through the savannas, he was left behind in the camp they had set a hundred or so kilometers from Nairobi. That was in the late 1800s and he hoped to continue with his journey as soon as he recovered. This did not happen and upon his recovery, he realized that the area where his camp was located was as good as any land he would find in the future. His camp was later to form part of what was to grow into the future town of Naivasha.

His father, Brian Trafford was to become one of the notorious members of the Happy Valley society, a group of rich settlers who enjoyed an easy life and partied daily. Their lives were now threatened by the Mau Maus and the colonial government had failed in protecting them. Each family had seconded one of its members to serve as a volunteer in the Vigilante Committee which was later absorbed into the Kenyan Regiment, popularly known as KR. Membership to KR was open not only to the white men but also to the Asians and Africans. However, the white men were favoured and gained the rank of an inspector on recruitment. For the Africans, none went beyond the rank of corporal.

Some six months earlier, his pregnant young bride had been killed in a daring attack by the Mau Mau insurgents while he was away on duty. On that fateful night, Raymond had received a distress call from a farmer who lived some twenty kilometers away. He left the comfort of his bed in a hurry towards the home of the family under attack. Little did he know that the wife he had left in bed, warm and safe, was to be a victim within thirty minutes of his departure. During that season, his mother had gone to England to nurse his grandmother who was on her deathbed while his father was spending the weekend in Nairobi.

As soon as he departed, the attackers cut-off the telephone line leaving the home at their mercy. They gathered all the workers and locked them in a store before heading to the cottage where the young bride slept, miles away from any neighbour. Uninterrupted, they killed the young pregnant woman before taking off with guns and other valuables from the home.

It was believed that he had been sent on a wild goose chase with an aim of luring him away from his home. He was being paid back for his cruelty in cracking down on the Mau Mau. Raymond was heartbroken and for days stayed locked in his cottage mourning his wife and the baby he would never hold in his hands.

When he emerged weeks later, he was adorned in his uniform ready to capture the criminals who had killed his wife. Whereas he had been said to be cruel before, this loss turned him into a monster. His life was dedicated to causing pain to his tormentors. The hate for the black people extended to his servants who he blamed for not protecting his bride on that fateful night. "These people are no different from those criminals we are fighting," he declared to his friends on many occasions.

Promotion in Her Majesty police service was earned by the zeal with which an officer defended her government. A zeal weighed by the brutality and the speed at which an officer sent the 'bloody Africans' to the camp. In front of a man with such credentials, my grandfather expected nothing but 'swift justice' that would earn him a place on the long list of prisoners to be transported in a few days' time. My grandmother told us many years later.

"What is your name?" Raymond, the Senior Police Inspector asked in a voice full of false friendliness.

"My name is Josphat Rucacu, *afande*," afande is the Kiswahili equivalent to 'Sir'. It was a title of respect used in addressing a police officer.

He went on to disclose that he was married and had three children, oldest among them going ten. On his education, he told him that he attended Gakarara Intermediate School located near Kandara in Fort Hall District (Fort Hall was to be renamed Murang'a District). His mention that he attended Alliance High School ignited a lot of interest.

"Rucacu, who were your classmates at Alliance?" The 'asking of a few questions' continued.

"They were many and came from all over the country afande,"

"I know that bit man. What I would like to hear is a mention of their names. Do not forget that I can phone and easily verify the information that you will give me," he paused ready to hear the list.

Having been a class prefect and having conducted the roll call every morning, remembering the names of his classmates was easy. As if holding the old register in his hands, he easily called out the names. Among them was Robert Matano, Kimani Muchoki, Julius Gikonyo Kiano, among others.

"Where are these people today?"

"I don't know where everyone is but some are working in Nairobi while others are pursuing studies abroad afande,"

"Why didn't you proceed abroad like the others?"

"I married soon after I left school and didn't want to leave my young family alone. I also come from a big family which needed my support afande,"

"Tell us about your activities with Mau Mau because this is the main reason that you could not proceed abroad for studies,"

"I am not involved in Mau Mau at all afande,"

"Rucacu you are an educated man and poised to play a bigger role in the development of this country. Tell us all you know and I will let you free to continue with your life. To me you do not appear like a criminal but you might have information which can assist in wiping out the bandits,"

"Afande, I know nothing other than what everybody hears,"

"What is it that everybody hears?"

"News that the Mau Mau have raided homes from time to time afande."

"That is not what I am looking for. I don't even need to read the papers or listen to the news to catch up with that. I am part of the news! What I need are names of who are the sympathizers of Mau Mau in this town or back in your village,"

"I know no one afande,"

"It's okay if that is the way you would like to play it. All I wanted was to be a gentleman in dealing with you but you seem not to value my gesture. There are other ways of getting the information from you, like leaving you with my boys for some time. May be by tomorrow you will be in a mood to cooperate,"

"Afande, I have told you all that I know,"

"Which is nothing but cow dung!"

As promised, the 'boys' were eager to work on him as soon as possible. For starters, they placed him in a small cell, whipped him, and only took a pause when his howling became deafening. This beating continued until he fainted. To revive him, they poured several buckets of water on him. Cold and wet, he spent the night in the small cell shivering and cursing the guards.

If anything, the beating hardened his resolve and he was ready to die rather than reveal the secrets of the Mau Mau. What would be the point of continued living if he betrayed his brothers who were fighting in the forest? He had taken an oath of supporting the movement and keeping its secrets no matter what befell him. Breaking such an oath could not only bring him and his family a curse, but could have his throat slit by the Mau Mau. That is how tough his choices were.

Like the many other cases she had seen or heard of, the arrest of her husband was most likely to be followed by her own. When and how this was to happen was what she could not tell. In the meantime, all that she could do was to prepare the children for this eventuality.

"You saw how they took your father? Those bad people might be coming for me as well," Julia my grandmother warned Ciku, my mother.

"What is going to happen to us mum?" Ciku had asked with concern.

"Nothing really though you will have to take care of your brothers. Mama Akinyi will look after you until Aunt Emily comes for you. She will make arrangements for your transport to your grandfather's home,"

"What about you and dad?"

"Don't worry. God will be watching over us,"

"Will they imprison you for a long time?" Ciku was eager to know.

"I do not know my dear. But whether short or long, we shall come back," she was plaiting her hair late in the night. For the first time in a day which had started with the dramatic arrest of her father, she got really worried over the future of their family. All along she knew that her father was innocent and assumed that he was not to spend more than a night in jail. To be faced with the possibility of her mother being taken away as well was a shocker and brought a new understanding of the magnitude of the problems ahead.

Ciku knew of children whose parents were in jail and the kind of life they led. Some were reduced to begging in the streets of Naivasha while others had been plucked from their homes and schools and transported to their rural home.

"Though I loved my grandparents very much, the prospects of starting a new life away from my parents and my known surroundings was not very appealing. What I really wanted was to continue with my life as it was," in a voice still heavy with emotions Ciku, my mother took over the narration.

It is then that she realized that this hurried hair plaiting late in the night, was part of the preparation of her mother's imminent arrest. She wanted to leave her hair clean and tidy. But for how long would her hair remain tidy? Long enough until arrival at their grandfather's home? Long enough until her mother came back? She had no answer to any of these nagging questions which was very frustrating.

"Mum what if they injure him?" These fears were genuine for she had heard of many prisoners who had returned home on crutches.

"All we can do Ciku is to pray that nothing like that happens to any of us." These assurances sounded thin, and both knew that her father was in the hands of a regime whose thinking was turned inside out, a people who believed that the harder a prisoner was to break, greater was the information held. Thus, they would torture a victim until he or she confessed to crimes not committed.

Where such a confession was hard to extract, they would extend their torture to the spouse of the prisoner. In many cases, this tactic worked and a prisoner would make a confession with an aim of saving his or her family.

"After spending a night on the floor of the waterlogged cell, your grandfather was cold, weak and could hardly stand on his feet. Half dragging him, they brought him to the office of the white police officer he had met the day before. He staggered towards the seat he had sat on the day before but he was steered away," effortlessly, Julia took over the narration from my mother. She had been told of what happened that morning by one of the arresting *ngati*.

"Do not set your dirty bottom on my chair," the police officer shouted in alarm. His dirty long trousers, dripping water could surely have ruined the seat. With nowhere to sit and too weak to stand, the wretched man slid down to the floor with his back supported by the wall. On any other day, such a floor could have been hard and cold for his bottom but not on this day, not after spending a whole night sitting on a wet floor. It almost felt luxurious especially with the sun that warmed the spot he had chosen to sit.

"Do you have anything to tell me today or are you still *kichwa ngumu* (hard headed)", his interrogator wanted to know as way of greetings.

"I am sorry but there is nothing to tell afande," in a weak voice my grandfather answered.

"Then there is no need of wasting my time on you. I know where to get the information. Your wife might be more cooperative than you are,"

The interview was over and to his relief they put him back into the common cell. He was in time for breakfast, which consisted of a bowl of porridge. The porridge was made from half cooked, rotten maize meal. It was a food made with an aim of dehumanizing the diner, a food that the dogs which were locked in another part of the compound could not touch. In fact, the dogs' menu was a hundred times better than that of the prisoners.

Though hungry, it was hard to push it down his throat but he had to, otherwise he would die of hunger. Sip by sip, he ate the porridge to the last drop.

"From one of his fellow prisoners, he learnt that at a fee, one of the guards would deliver urgent messages to the outside world. Such a contact was important for the prisoners were allowed no visitors. It was through this guard that I learnt of my planned arrest and his impending transfer to Manyani in a few days' time". My grandmother paused and took a break to visit the latrine.

The night was lit by a half moon and she easily picked her way to the latrine which was built in one corner of the compound. Though having been in Kandara for almost four months, I still dreaded the nights which were at times so dark that you could hardly see anything. In such a night, I imagined all sorts of monsters which could grab and drag me to their lair as their dinner if I went outside.

I could therefore never venture out of the house alone and even if in the company of someone else, I clung on that person which at times was irritating. It is only my grandmother who understood my fears and she would escort me to the toilet and patiently wait for me to complete my business. This was absurd because my grandmother was not very strong and was bent with age. If a monster attacked us, it was very likely that we could have been consumed together.

On this night, I had a while ago heard the cries of a hyena from across the ridge. I assumed that she too heard it but still casually ventured out of the safety of the house.

She amazed me and could not understand the source of her courage. All I could do was to pray that nothing horrible happened as I waited for her at the door of the house scanning the moon lit darkness.

Chapter Seven

When Njoroge, a middle aged man and a *ngati* at Naivasha police station, removed his uniform and wore his civilian clothes, his menacing appearance disappeared. Soft spoken, clad in a shirt and trousers freshly pressed, the man could have been mistaken for a local teacher.

Though harsh while on duty, the man sympathized with the Mau Mau and on many occasions frustrated the activities of the colonial police. The only problem was that his assistance came at a fee which in my grandfather's case, covered the piece of paper and the pencil with which he wrote a note to my grandmother.

"I can remember the evening when the note was delivered very well. We had just taken our dinner and were preparing for bed. The knock came as a surprise for no visitors were expected at such a time in the evening. Above all, it was during the curfew hours which started at six in the evening to six in the morning and all natives were supposed to be indoors,"

"Who is it?" My grandmother had asked in a surprised voice.

"I am a friend and have a letter from your husband,"

The mention of my grandfather's name was magical and she unbolted the heavy door with trembling hands. She was seized by a worry that something terrible had happened to him. Holding the door with one hand and its frame with the other, she faced the stranger whose face was poorly lit by the weak glow of the lamp behind her. She could not remember having seen his face anywhere and in an anxious voice greeted him.

"With my husband away, I had no intention of welcoming a man into the house especially at night.

Meanwhile the children crowded behind me, eager to see the night visitor," Julia had gone on with the narration after her safe visit to the toilet.

"Sorry for calling on you at such an hour but the message I have could not wait," he explained.

"It's okay. We were still awake."

He handed over the note which Julia strained to read with the weak light. The writing was that of her husband and in an instant her feelings towards the stranger changed. "You better come in," she welcomed the night visitor and at the same time moved nearer the lamp. She read and re-read the note before lifting a face clouded with worry.

The note was written in Kikuyu language and said;

"I am well though the future looks uncertain. I have information that we are being moved to Manyani detention camp in a few days and that you might be arrested as well. Make arrangements with your friends to take the children if you are arrested. Take care of yourself and greet the children for me. Burn this note as soon as you read it".

"How did you get this note?" My grandmother demanded with curiosity.

"I am a guard at the station. You do not seem to remember me but I am one of the guards who was here the other morning,"

"Ooh, no wonder I thought your voice was familiar. How is he?"

"He is okay and sent his greetings. He also told me that you would give me some cash for risking my life in delivering this note,"

"Where do I get the cash to give you?"

"I will leave that to you. Give me what you can afford,"

Julia disappeared behind the curtain that shielded the sleeping area from the rest of the room and after a short while, came with some coins. Without even counting, the stranger who had by now introduced himself as Njoroge pocketed the cash and stood up ready to go. "Is there anything that I can tell your husband?"

"Just greet him. Tell him that we are well,"

"Sleep well and sorry for the troubles that you are facing,"

"Just a minute let me escort you to the gate. Ciku do not let your brothers follow me. It's cold outside,"

After walking a few steps out of the house, my grandmother started digging for details she could not have asked for in the hearing of the children. What she heard was horrifying and went back into the house more worried about the welfare of her husband. As soon as she locked the door, Ciku and the other children anxiously mobbed her wanting to know what the letter said.

"It is from your father. He says that he is okay and greets you," she reassured them.

"When is he coming back?" Ciku wanted to know.

"He will not be away for long,"

"Will he bring me a present?" Mwaniki the youngest asked.

"Of course baby, he says that he will bring you a sweet if you remain a good boy,"

"What about me?" Muna sensing that he might be left out when the presents arrive claimed his share.

"He will bring sweets for you too,"

"I prefer the ones with a stick," Muna specified the kind of sweets he wanted for a present.

Assured that their father was well and that each would receive a present, the children went to bed and in a short while the house was quiet. Julia was left sitting, lost in thought over the future of her children and husband.

She was not very much worried about herself but was really bothered over her husband who was a major operative of the Mau Mau.

He was one of the major conduits of information and letters from Nairobi and areas around Naivasha. As a clerk at the railway station, this was easy and no one could suspect his underground activities. The messages he received were easily passed on through the man who delivered milk every morning. It was a very well-coordinated secret activity.

Julia's was concerned over what would happen to the children if she was also arrested. This was because Naivasha was far from their ancestral home in Fort Hall. Other than this, most of her neighbours were from different tribes and faraway places. Though not from her tribe, her neighbours were friendly and could take care of the children. However, she wanted someone who could deliver them to their grandfather in Kandara.

Her hope lay in Emily, a close friend and a village mate who together with her husband worked in the home of Lord Delamere. This was a short distance from the town center and she would send a word through the milkman in the morning. Later, she walked across to Mama Akinyi's house and briefed her on what was likely to happen the following morning. She also asked her to send news of her arrest through the milk man in case they came for her early in the morning.

"Do not worry over the children. I will take care of them until your friend comes," mama Akinyi assured her.

"That night I did not go to bed because I had a lot of things to do before the new day came. All my labours of that night were guided by the Agikuyu proverb *muthii ndoimbikaga irigu*, which roughly means, he who is to travel does not leave bananas roasting. Like this proverbial traveller, I was likely to travel the next day and knew not when I would be coming back."

"My first task was to remove from under the bed

the wooden box that held our clothes and other important items. I pulled out a dress I had made for you," she was referring to my mother.

The dress was made of some light cotton material with flowery patterns in a light blue and green colour. It was decorated with buttons in the front with its neckline bound by a shiny satin ribbon whose two ends extended for a few inches and were tied together like some form of a bow tie. On its waist, a broad band was sewn from the sides and by tying it into a knot, the dress which was two or three sizes bigger for Ciku could be easily gathered. This dress was the latest product of her treasured sewing machine that occupied one corner of the one roomed house. It was a dress Ciku wore with pride because no one else had such a dress in their estate.

From the same box came a small wooden square box which was around six inches in length. The only access to its belly was through a thin slit on one of the faces through which the family savings were kept. When the need to access the money inside arose, one had to forcefully ply-out one of its sides.

"Becky it was your grandfather who usually opened the piggy bank and later hammered back the cover. That night he was away and with impatience, I clumsily crashed the box with a hammer. Within a short time, several currency notes and quite a number of coins lay spewed on the floor. In those days, some of the coins were made of copper and had a hole in the center. As for the bank notes, the imposing portrait of Queen Elizabeth dominated their faces. I counted the coins and tied them together with a piece of cloth while placing the notes on one side,"

"I undid the hem of the dress and using pins arranged the notes all along the old hem. I then sewed it back and ironed the new hem to make it look even. Without closer examination, one could hardly notice the new lining of currency notes. I gave the same treatment to another dress and all of my family treasure in currency notes had a new home. The coins went to the bottom of the *kiondo* which you were to carry your things in,"

"I also removed a few shorts and shirts for your brothers and together with the moneyed dresses placed them in the kiondo. Your father's suits and uniforms which hang on the wall behind the curtain went into the wooden box as well. Emily was to take care of the box and everything else in case I was arrested," Julia, my grandmother narrated while facing my mother.

At some point of her packing, she re-lit the charcoal burner and placed a pot of maize and beans on it. By morning there was enough *githeri* for the children to eat as they liked for the next few days.

"Ciku, Ciku, I gently shook you awake," my grandmother continued while pointing at my mother.

"I did not bother with your brothers who slept on the couch. Lost to the world and snoring slightly, you continued sleeping as I continued shaking and calling your name,"

"Wake up Ciku," scratching her hands and feet from the mosquito bites, Ciku eventually arose and half sat on the mat.

"What time is it mum?" Ciku could remember asking my grandmother and as if running in a relay race, my mother seamlessly took over the narration.

"It's still dark and too early to go to school," Ciku complained.

"I know but just wake up," my grandmother urged.

"What is it then?"

"I would like you to take some tea as we talk," she was now fully alert and ready to listen to Julia. Fears that something had happened to her father while she slept heightened her anxiety.

"Is it about my father?"

"Yes it has to do with your father,"

"Has something terrible happened to him?" The many tales she had heard of people dying mysteriously while in police cells raised a storm in her young heart.

"No my dear," my grandmother reassured her. "Nothing has happened to him. But we should continue praying for him,"

"Will you take us to see him sometimes?"

"That will not be possible my dear. They do not allow anybody to see the prisoners. All we can do is pray," she explained while handing her a cup of tea.

"Would you like some *githeri*?" Ciku shook my head.

In those days, their breakfast was usually porridge together with any other food that remained after dinner. It was only on special occasions like on Christmas day that they got tea and bread. This was not a Christmas morning and getting tea and githeri could have been a luxury under different circumstances. However, it was too early and Ciku had no appetite. She sipped her tea with a mind faraway.

"You saw the man who came here before you slept?" Ciku nodded.

"He informed me that they would be coming for me tomorrow," anyone eavesdropping on them, could have thought that the person coming for her would be taking her for a picnic. However, the picture of how they would 'come' for her was clear in Ciku's mind because she had seen with embarrassment her father walking on his toes. Anytime she remembered that scene, anger rose in her chest.

"How were these brutal men going to handle my mother? Since she wore a dress, how were they going to make her walk on her toes?" Ciku was curious but whatever happened, she could not bear the idea of anyone touching her mother and would do anything to prevent it.

"I would like you to take care of your brothers when I am gone. Always remember that you are the oldest in the family and that God is watching over us," that night, my grandmother had paused for a moment and caressed Ciku's hair which was now done in corn rows which ended at the back of her head.

"You see, these two dresses," she was pointing to the dresses she had removed from the *kiondo*.

"I have hidden money in their hems and waist bands. Until you arrive at your grandmother's home, keep wearing them. Never remove them or allow anyone to wash them for you. If they are dirty and needs washing, do them yourself. Another thing, never tell anyone of what is hidden in them, not even your brothers. This is a secret between the two of us,"

"Will I be wearing both of them?" Ciku asked while caressing the hems. As her mother had said, they were smooth and showed no signs of the treasure in them.

"If travelling, wear both of them,"

"What about when we go to school?" She saw a potential problem for she had to wear a uniform to school.

"Ciku I have to tell you the truth," she paused for a moment as she chose her words carefully. The light in the room was not very bright but Ciku could see the pain on her face. It was as if she was not decided on whether to continue or not. "I do not think it will be possible for you to continue with your schooling while we are away," the tears Ciku had been holding back were now loose. Like sap flowing from a cut on a banana stem, they freely flowed. She could not imagine missing classes especially when the examinations were this near.

"What is likely to happen is that you will be transported to your grandparents' home in Kandara within a short time.

That is what they do with children whose parents are in jail,"

"But *Mami*, can't we run away and hide?" She tearfully wanted to know.

"It's' not possible my dear,"

"We can move to another town like Nakuru where my father has friends," Ciku was getting excited with this possibility.

"We can do that yes, but how are we going to survive? They will have every policeman looking for us as soon as they realize we have escaped. Ciku, it's not possible and they will eventually arrest me and claim that I have something to hide,"

"But Mum, what is going to happen to us if you never return?" She was worried that something terrible she dared not put in words could happen to her parents.

"Nothing will happen to us. We will come back. Just keep an eye on your brothers. Make sure they wear a sweater in the evening and when it is cold. That way you will keep colds and flu away. Also make sure that they finish their food. Once you arrive at your grandparents' place, all will be well."

After more questions and assurances, Ciku was calm and ready to face a future with her parents away. She understood her new responsibilities and though worried, hoped to keep her brothers safe till her parents returned.

Chapter Eight

It was approaching dawn when Ciku went back to bed and after much tossing and turning, fell asleep. She dreamt that Mwaniki, her youngest brother was crying and asking for his mother. While holding and swaying him on her lap, she sang a lullaby that always worked magic in soothing him to sleep.

"Ooh koma mwana-ii
Nduutige kurira
Nyukwa niathire-ii
Nandagacoka ringi-ii"

Translated it says;

"Ooh baby sleep
Please stop crying
Your mother travelled
To a distant land
She will never come back again."

As predicted, the boy fell asleep and she gently placed him on her parent's bed. This was a disturbing dream that sort of confirmed her fears that her parents would never come back. She later dreamt that they were coming from the market with her mum. Ciku was carrying a basket of vegetables. A distance from their house, she heard her brothers crying and knew that something was wrong. She put down her basket and rushed in the direction of the cries. No matter how hard she tried, she could not gain a hold on the slippery steep path. Many times she fell and slid back to the bottom of the path.

In frustration, she started wailing asking for help. Unfortunately, no matter how much she shouted, no sound came from her throat. It was as if somebody was strangling her.

She arose to the cry of her baby brother who was having a nightmare of his own. A little soothing from her mother calmed him down and he soon went back to sleep.

The night or what was left of it turned out to be very short for hardly had she lain down again that loud urgent knocks on the door arose her. Whoever was knocking was in a hurry and wanted the door opened immediately. She was disoriented and took a moment to rise from her mat.

What followed was an urgent call from her mother. "Ciku, Ciku, wake up, there is no time to waste," her mother anxiously whispered. Meanwhile, the knocking continued.

"Who is it?" Julia shouted without opening the door.

"The Police, open the door immediately," whoever had been knocking answered.

"I will in a short while but I need to dress up, wait a moment," she pleaded.

"By this time, my mother had managed to light the lamp and dress, ready to face the policemen. My two brothers were also awake and in fear of whoever was on the other side of the door, started crying. Having witnessed the arrest of my father a few days before, their fear was valid. They knew that the mission of whoever was knocking was not a friendly one," my mother, in those days known as Ciku took over the narration from my grandmother.

"Muna, the boy born after me, the boy who had fought against the arrest of my father, the self-appointed muscle man and the family protector in the absence of my father, was ready for the policemen. His first task was to ensure that the door was double bolted, and reinforced by placing a chair as wedge against it.

"*Ko, ko, ko,*" the loud knocking continued. Whoever was knocking was no longer using his knuckles but a baton. He was getting impatient.

"Open the door or we break it down," he threatened.

"Just a moment, I am opening. Let me dress the children," Julia pleaded. She knew that the police had to wait for the door and its frames were made of metal while the walls were made of bricks. Even if they went on with their threats, it could have taken time to break in. Other than this, Muna had pushed the table and some chairs to the door as enforcement.

"Now Ciku remember what I told you last night," Julia whispered. "Prepare some porridge for your brothers and do not cry. I will now open the door."

Though warned against crying, all the children were not only crying but their wailing filled the cold morning. Mwaniki, the smallest was in her mother's arms and refused to be put down.

"Woman, open the door this moment!" The shouting accompanied by the knocking continued.

"Muna, remove these things from the door. I do not want them to destroy the door. We will need it to lock our things in,"

Reluctantly, Muna removed the blockade and unbolted the door. Her mother pulled it half open but continued holding the shatter with one hand. She also stood on the little opening while the small boy nestled on her hip. Behind her, Muna and Ciku struggled for space through which to see what was happening.

"*Mama wewe iko fikiri sisi iko wakati wa kupoteza?*" in his trademark broken Kiswahili, the white policeman was asking Julia why she thought that they had time to waste.

"My mother had no answer to this question and

in confusion, continued standing in her position with the door still held in her hand,"

"Move out of the way. We would like to come in," the policeman ordered.

"I do not have enough seats for all of you. Maybe you should tell me what you want from here," she innocently answered.

"We do not want to sit we are searching the house,"

"What are you looking for? It would be easier for me to give it to you. I know where everything is kept in this house,"

"Give us the guns you keep for the Mau Mau,"

"If that is what you are looking for, then you are wasting your time for a second time,"

"Get out of the way woman. We don't have time for idle talk."

My mother did not move from the door way thus literally blocking their way. In all the homes they had visited in their investigations (including their last visit to this very home), this was the first time they were being denied entry. All their victims (men and women) were always meek and ready to do as told. Patiently, his African policemen waited for the orders to storm the house.

"Boys go ahead and do your work," the white policeman ordered. There was a moment of hesitation as they looked at the woman who blocked their way. It was as if they were asking themselves whether to request her to allow them in, or to simply push her aside. Pushing her could have been easy but how do you push a woman holding a baby and heavy with another one?

"I said move on," he shouted at his colleagues.

"Rather than face the fury of their boss, the policemen pushed Julia aside and like hungry safari ants, swarmed the house in search of the imaginary weapons. In a blink of an eye, the clothes which my mother had spent precious time packing littered the floor while the sofa set was torn in all the possible places where a gun could have been kept. Jumbled on the floor was the curtain that divided the room into two and bedding.”

The number of the policemen involved in the search and the size of the room they were searching left no space for a mother and her children. To avoid being trampled with their *kabunja ndua*, my grandmother led the children out and in disbelief watched the second violation of their home. Their actions were like those of drunkard urinating on a sacred tree!

As soon as it had started the search came to an end. One by one, they streamed out of the house with no guns, or anything that could have implicated Julia.

“Pass the baby to the girl. You are coming with us,” one of the policeman ordered.

“Like in the arrest of my father a few days ago, the Land Rover was parked in the compound and my mother was ordered to climb in. Pushing the wailing boy into my hands, she calmly climbed into the Land Rover leaving me cuddling Mwaniki while holding Muna’s hand,” my mother retold.

“Remember what I said,” those were the final words before she was driven away. Like turning off a tap, the source of her tears was dry. She was left consoling her brothers who were still wailing.

Chapter Nine

By planting the toes of one of her bare foot on the ground, Ciku was able to raise one side of her hip. On this raised and twisted hip, her baby brother nestled. She then wound one of her hands below his shoulders for support. With the other hand, she held Muna's wrist.

"Muna was struggling for his freedom, but after witnessing the scene of the arrest of my father, I had no intention of releasing him, at least not immediately," with a faraway look, my mother remembered the incidence that occurred more than fifty years ago.

As soon as the Land Rover disappeared in a cloud of dust, she let Muna free and like someone stung by bees, he took to his heels in pursuit. Ciku was not very bothered for she knew that this was a fruitless exercise for the vehicle was too fast to catch up with.

Just like Muna was never going to catch up with the Land Rover, Ciku in turn could never catch up with him, especially while bearing the weight of her brother who clung to her like *maramata*. *Maramata* is a type of a hitchhiker seed whose hooks and barb cling to clothes and hairy animal coats. Thus, with the weight on her waist, she followed him in a hurried clumsy walk.

There she was, a whole ten years old girl with a dignity to preserve, trying to run after a brother who was making a fool of himself. It was a race that was drawing unhealthy attention from the other children in the estate though through the slightly opened doors, and was likely to be breaking news in the school that morning.

Such a story would be whispered from one ear to the next, and by the end of the day, every one would be looking at her in a funny way. She knew that the bullies would use this incident in teasing and making her life in school as uncomfortable as they could. For the first time, she was glad that she would not be attending school that morning.

"Running out of breath and with my brother bouncing on my hip like someone riding a horse, I run, for this was the only way to bring to an end this embarrassing episode. Fortunately (or do I say unfortunately), Muna tripped on a stone outcrop on the road and in a blink of an eye I saw him flying high in the air. Like in the movies, he rolled a number of times before coming to rest in a dusty heap in the middle of the road, motionless."

Ciku was gripped by a new fear that Muna, one of the brothers she had sworn to protect the night before, was dead. Even for a girl with a dignity to preserve, this fear was far greater than that of the gossiping that her undignified gallop would draw. She stopped briefly and unglued herself from her baby brother who was a hindrance to her movement and like a mad girl, ran to where Muna lay.

Equally worried by the fate of his brother, Mwaniki the baby brother who she had just unglued herself from, ran after her, and in a moment both knelt around Muna.

"His teary eyes were closed but from the rise and fall of his chest assumed that he was still breathing. This did not reduce my worry for I could not tell whether he was breathing for the last time or not," my mother continued with the narration.

"Muna, Muna, wake up," she anxiously called while shaking him by the shoulder. She got no response other than his shallow breathing.

"Can you hear me?" With tears loose again and streaming down her face, Ciku called. She got no answer and she truly thought that her brother was dying, if not already dead. She had never seen a dead body but knew that stillness was one sign of death.

Ciku was worried, very worried.

She lifted one of his hands and when she let it free, if fell back on the dusty road like a piece of wood. This was enough evidence that her brother was dead. With no care of what her playmates would say, Ciku wailed in a loud voice calling for help.

"That morning, kneeling on that dusty road, weeping and with my face buried in the chest of my dying brother, I blamed God for my troubles. He had allowed tragedy after tragedy to follow me. In less than a week my parents were in jail, my brother lay dead in the middle of a rough road, my schooling had come to an end, and this morning I would be the subject of gossip. What was I supposed to do? Cry to the same God who had allowed all these to happen? I was confused as I held my brother's shoulder, shaking him back to life,"

"God is supposed to be my friend, as I had been taught at an early age. Friends were supposed to be caring and supportive to one another and if a friend turned against me, I simply 'unfriended' him or her. What was I supposed to do to a God who had turned against me?"

Presently, Mwaniki was crouching over his brother sobbing with tears streaming down his face and joining the messy mucus issuing from his nose unrestrained. Any time he tried to sweep it away with the back of his hand left a messy smear all the way to his ears. He was wailing and at the same time calling out his brother's name.

"Muna, Muna please do not die," Mwaniki pleaded.

"As if in response to Mwaniki's pleas, Muna slowly opened his eyes as if coming from a deep sleep. I do not think I can get the right words to describe my feelings at that moment. It was a joy that soothingly flooded my heart. Though I had doubted His faithfulness as a friend a moment ago, I thanked Him (Who else would I have thanked anyway?) for He had seen the pain I was in, and came to my rescue even before I could utter a word in prayers," my mother told of her painful past with a smile.

"Come on," Ciku urged while pulling him to a sitting position. She then examined his big toe whose nail was torn apart and bleeding.

He was fully awake and he tearfully told her that he could have caught up with the Land Rover had he not tripped and fell. This was of course not true, but she had no wish of contradicting a brother who had just risen from the dead.

"That car was not as fast as a hare," she soothed him by reminding him of his prowess, especially in their last hunting expedition where he had pursued a hare and captured it with his bare hands.

"I know that as girls aged ten years, I had every right of joining my brothers in continued sobbing but I didn't do so because my eyes had gone dry again. Maybe I had shed all the tears that my eye could store!"

When they took her mother away, she felt a chill down her spine and for a moment her body shook. She then felt weighed down as if a heavy load had been placed on her shoulders. It is then that she realized that the leadership of her family rested on her shoulders. This was a heavy responsibility and as such, there were things she could do, and things she could not do. One of them was crying with her brothers. She was to be strong and sooth them whenever they cried.

She pulled Mwaniki and Muna to a standing position and led them to their house which was a chaotic pile of their belongings. Presently, some of their neighbours joined them and within a short while rearranged the furniture into their normal positions. Mama Akinyi also dressed Muna's bleeding toe with a rag.

"Ciku do not worry. They have no reason of locking

up your mother," Mama Akinyi reassured as she served them hot porridge she had brought from her house.

"But Mama Akinyi, Mum told us that we will be transported," to be transported was the term used for forceful removal of a family from one place to another by the white man.

"I do not think so but even if it happens, always remember that my house is also your house. I will care for you until they come back."

******

Sitting on the steps to their house, one could see for quite a distance the stretch of the road that connected their estate with the rest of the town. On many occasions they had sat on these steps waiting for their mother who at least once a week, went to the market. Anytime a figure of a woman appeared from a distance, their hopes would be lifted, and they would think that it was their mother bearing her heavy basket home. Their imagination took them right inside her basket, which always held some mouth-watering items like ripe bananas, oranges, sugar cane or even a surprise loaf of bread.

As the figure came nearer, they would realize that it was not their mother and their hopes would come crashing down. Their spirits would be down for just a short moment for another figure would soon appear. They would play this game until their mother came and they would all rush to her and take the basket from her hands. Once inside the house, she would waste no time as she shared out whatever presents she had brought.

On the day Julia was arrested, Ciku spent the better part of the day on those steps. Her two brothers were involved in one of their many games but from time to time their attention would be directed to the road that would bring their mother home. On her part, she had cleaned the floor of their house and washed the few utensils they had used. She then tried to do some revision but like her brothers, her attention would be drawn to the road.

"Earlier in the morning, Mama Akinyi had told us not to bother cooking for she would provide us with all the meals of the day. This she generously did on that day and for the rest of the week we were alone in the house. She would leave us alone in between the meals though she would come over whenever she heard our baby brother cry. Up to today, I do not know how one can repay back such generosity," my mother concluded.

To their disappointment, their mother did not appear on the road. Neither did she knock on their door that evening. Dejected, the three children piled on their parent's bed and huddled together for warmth and security. For a long time, Ciku lay sleepless listening for any movement around the house. Whenever she heard a strange sound outside, she would in fear lie still like a log. Those were the days when, leopards, hyenas and even lions roamed the plains around Naivasha and in many other parts of Kenya.

Though the other children went to school, Ciku and Muna stayed home and took care of their brother while waiting for their mother's return. Ciku's hopes of her mother's release were higher than those of the release of her father. Not that she loved her mother more than her father but somehow she felt that life could still go on even without his presence as long as her mother was around. This feeling could have grown from the many occasions he was away for days, working in faraway stations.

Their mother did not return the next day. Neither on the days that followed. However, their hope that she would return at any time remained high and they maintained the routine of their first day. Mama Akinyi, with the support of other neighbours continued feeding them with the main meals, but in between, they visited the pot of githeri or drank the milk which was delivered every morning.

This monotony was broken by a visit from Aunt Emily on the fourth day. She brought news on the welfare of their parents. "Your parents are being held at the police station but there are plans to transport them to Manyani soon," Aunt Emily informed them.

"Where is Manyani?" Muna wanted to know.

"Manyani is a detention camp very far from here,"

"What is a detention camp?"

"It's a place where the white man keeps some of the people fighting their rule,"

"But my father and mother are not fighters. He works at the station while my mother stays at home," Muna exonerated their parents.

"I know that Muna but they suspect that your parents are secretly assisting the fighters in the forest,"

"That isn't true and they should release my dad and mum immediately," Muna concluded while shaking his head from side to side.

"I know they are and they will be released soon. Before that happens, all you have to do is take care of one another and listen to what Ciku tells you. I will come again on Sunday,"

That evening while taking dinner in the now crowded house of mama Akinyi, Ciku wanted to know more about Manyani. "Aunt Emily said that my parents will be taken to Manyani,"

"She told me too,"

"Where is Manyani?"

"Manyani is a jail that holds thousands and thousands of prisoners. It is located in a remote part of the savannah, out of the town of Voi. It is far removed from any human settlement that escape from this jail is hard. An escapee has to walk miles and miles of bush inhabited by many wild animals including 'the man eaters of Tsavo.'

"Man eaters of Tsavo? I have never heard of such an animal. How does it look like?" Muna, with his keen interest in animals wanted to know.

"That's just a name given to lions in that area. It refers to a pack of notorious lions which had developed a deep appetite for human flesh during the building of the railway line," she had pointed to the general direction of the railway line that passed behind their house.

"Ooh, I know my father will not attempt such a risky escape," in amazement Muna saw the uselessness of a prisoner escaping from jail only to fall into the jaws of a hungry lion.

Chapter Ten

The day that her mother was arrested was the turning point in Ciku's life. That is the morning that her mother placed Mwaniki in her hands. This was a responsibility that went beyond holding the young boy for a while; it was the responsibility of holding the family together until her mother's return. At that time she didn't know what was to happen in the future but believed that her parents would come back and that their life would continue as usual.

That morning, she went through the amount of food they had in store and in her estimation, the most they could live without relying on their neighbours and friends was roughly a month. In store was dry maize and beans which her mother had just harvested from a piece of land she cultivated at the edge of the railway station. But even with her limited housekeeping experience, she knew that they needed more than maize and beans to survive.

Behind their housing block, her mother cultivated a small vegetable garden for their daily use. These plus what they had in stock made the basic foods they ate most of the days. From time to time she would throw in cowpeas or any other grains which were readily available. Those were the days when things like rice and *chapattis* were luxuries they could only dream of and featured in their menu on Christmas day.

For their breakfast they usually took a calabash of freshly cooked porridge made with millet or sorghum flour. At times, her mother would add some milk which made it very delicious and they would take it until their stomachs ballooned like a tick.

She knew that milk was essential to her young

brother and intended to continue receiving the supply until the end of the month. By that time she believed that her parents would have come back and would take care of the monthly bill.

While taking the inventory, she was angry with the police officers who had broken their big bellied gourd. Its content of sour porridge could have been a good drink in between the meals and could have boosted their stocks in a big way.

For the week they lived alone, they continued living as if their mother had gone to the market and that she would be coming back soon. They took their meals at Mama Akinyi's house but in between cooked porridge to fill in the gaps. The rest of their time was spent playing in the courtyard just like before.

One of the games that she used to like was that of playing adults in which she organized her brothers and other children into a family unit. Each would take a role in the family. Being the oldest, she usually took the role of a mother while her brother Muna, or any other big boy in the compound would take the role of a father. This was a game that they would play for hours.

In the week they were alone, this was one game that she could not bring herself to play and did not have to play anyway! She was experiencing the role she could have taken live, and she was not enjoying it at all. How she wished that the whole thing was a game, or even a dream and that she would wake up in the morning and find her mother preparing breakfast!

Though they lived alone, they were under the watchful eyes of their neighbours. This was in line with African tradition that children belong to the community. This meant that it was the responsibility of the neighbours to ensure that they were fed and safe. From time to time, some other woman in the estate, other than mama Akinyi would prepare extra food and deliver it to their house, and if any of her brothers was crying, the concerned neighbours would walk over and find out what the problem was.

During the visit by Aunt Emily, she informed them that she could not take them-in because she lived in the compound of her employer and her work was involving. She woke up early in the morning and spent the whole day at her work. Though she did not tell them, she thought that bringing three children belonging to a Mau Mau to her house could have compromised her relationship with her employer. That aside, and from Ciku's assessment, they were better off in the estate compared with living in a compound of a man who was literally keeping her parents as prisoners.

Aunt Emily promised to come and spend Sunday night, but Ciku could not tell if she ever came or not. If she did, the visit was a waste of time for they were transported a day after her visit. Towards the evening of that day, an African policeman passed by their house and told them to get ready for they were to be transported to their grandfather's home in Fort Hall, the following day.

"Whereas such news of an impending visit to my grandparents could have raised excitement a few days ago, this visit was unwelcome. It was a visit that was to take us away from where my parents would be returning to, once they were released. What we didn't know at that moment was that my parents were very many miles away. My father had been moved to Manyani while my mother had been moved to Wang'uru center. Wang'uru is located a few miles from Embu town."

Though she was not keen on going away, she went ahead and prepared her brothers for the eventual move and informed Mama Akinyi of the new development. Early the next morning, Mama Akinyi prepared a big heap of *ngunja gutu* for them and packed it in a dish. This a form of ugali cooked together with vegetables. Ugali is maize flour mixed with hot water and cooked until it turns into a sort of thick bread. She told them to eat the food sparingly because the journey would be long and it may be hours before they got anything else to eat.

She also assisted in packing the few clothing items they were to carry in one of her mother's sisal bags. When the black Land Rover that had been used in taking her parents away arrived, they were ready and handed the keys to their house to Mama Akinyi. Their destination was the police station where they were moved into a lorry together with other children whose parents were in jail.

The high sided lorry was a perfect means of transport for potatoes and cabbages which grew abundantly on the hills beyond Naivasha. It could also have been ideal in moving the fattened bullocks from the ranches to the slaughter houses in Nairobi. However, it was a very unfriendly means of transport for human beings, especially children who were not tall enough to hold onto the bars which held the tarpaulin in place.

With nothing to hold onto or sit on, the young passengers sat on its dusty floor littered with manure, or simply stood and yielded to the motion of the lorry, as its crazy driver braked or hit pot holes.

"Though I knew that our journey was long, my expectations were that having departed early, sunset would find us at my grandparent's home at the worst. In the first one hour or so, the drive was smooth in terms of speed but still very uncomfortable until a short distance after Uplands when our lorry broke down. There was a lot of consultation in front of the lorry as the driver peered under its hood," my mother continued with the narration which had gone on far beyond my bedtime. However I was determined to hear the story to the end.

They were allowed to alight and relieve themselves in

the nearby bushes but the guards stood nearby all through. This was not a very comfortable atmosphere, especially for a girl her age. There is a certain freedom that a girl needs to do some of these things. How did they expect her body to function normally when a man with a gun stood within a hearing distance? She had her own gun to fire and preferred doing it in private! Albeit in difficulty, she relieved herself and headed back to the lorry.

It was in the mid-morning and she assumed that the necessary repairs would be done without delay and that they would still arrive as expected. The mechanic who had to come with the spare part all the way from Naivasha worked on the engine for hours with little success. Sunset was approaching and it was getting dark but the man was still under the lorry.

Idle, tired, cold and hungry, they had spent the day huddled in the lorry. One could alight and do whatever business that needed doing in the nearby bushes but would then be herded back into the lorry. In short, though not declared, they were prisoners whose rights for free movement had been taken away.

"We had consumed the *ngunja gutu* sparingly as advised but with so many hungry souls around us, we had to share some of it. However, I set a little aside for Mwaniki,"

Though the lorry was now repaired, the fall of darkness doomed the journey for no white man would dare drive on this stretch of the road under the cover of darkness. It was too dangerous and an ambush by the Mau Mau most certain. They were driven to the nearby Uplands police station where they were put in a cell no bigger than the lorry they had been travelling in. They were crowded but this time around they didn't complain for they needed to keep one another warm. With no blanket to cover them and on an empty stomach she spent the most miserable night of her life.

Chapter Eleven

One of the methods the colonial government kept the people in the villages under control and informed was through the *baraza* (public meeting). The crier would walk the paths of the village announcing the upcoming baraza. Every adult was expected to attend with fines or even imprisonment imposed on any absentee.

It was in one of these *baraza* that their grandfather came to know that Ciku and the other children would be dropped at High Level near Thika the following day. Not knowing the exact time of their arrival the old man was at the bus stop early in the morning. He packed his bicycle under the mugumo tree and waited, though they were still stuck more than a hundred kilometers away. Towards 5.30 pm and with the evening curfew approaching, he cycled to his brother's house in Thika and spent the night.

Early the next morning, he passed by Thika police station and inquired about the children who were to have been transported the previous day. He was informed that they had received a signal from Uplands informing them that the lorry transporting the children had set off and would be arriving in the mid-morning.

"Ciku," her grandfather called out as soon as they alighted from the lorry. It was a relief to see the familiar friendly face of her grandfather who appeared to have changed little. She had last seen him before Mwaniki was born which was close to four years.

"Who is this?" He asked when he came to Mwaniki.

"This is our other brother Mwaniki," she introduced him.

From the basket that hung from the bicycle handles, he produced some bananas which he passed around. As they ate, they gave him an update of their journey; how they had spent a cold night on the road after the lorry broke down somewhere in the forest and of how they had slept huddled together in the bone-chilling night, hungry.

"Do not worry over the hardships you have gone through, the most important thing is that you have arrived safely," their grandfather had assured.

Setting the bicycle on its stands, *Guka* (grandfather) lifted Mwaniki and placed him on the back of the bicycle. "Hold on to these", he instructed him to hold on the springs below his seat. He then assisted Ciku sitting behind Mwaniki. All through, she doubted whether the bicycle would carry all of them.

"I was sitting close to my brother with my legs hanging on either side of the bicycle and there was hardly any space between us. Parts of my bottom spilled over from the carrier. Muna was eventually raised and sat on the crossbar of the bicycle and instructed to hold the middle of the handlebar. He then hung our basket on one side of the steering handle and slowly set us on motion,"

With their tummies full of ripe bananas and the warm company of Guka, they hardly noticed the bumpy ride of ten kilometers journey to Kandara. He cycled slowly, precariously balancing the basket on one side of the handles and his three passengers.

Along the way, he pointed out the various coffee plantations they passed by. "This is *Mahuti* and the one we left behind is *Wangu*. Beyond the river are other plantations owned by the Europeans."

******

"These are your cousins from Naivasha. Do you remember Uncle Rucacu? The one who works with the railway and came to visit a month ago? These are his children and they will be staying with us," on arrival, her grandfather introduced them to a girl who was still in shock. At that moment, Ciku could not explain her odd reaction to their presence but something deep inside told her that this is one place they were not welcome, at least by the girl before them.

"This is Jecinta a daughter to your Aunt Rebecca who works in Nairobi. Ciku, what class are you in?" Her grandfather continued with the introductions.

"Class four," Ciku answered

"I thought so. Jecinta is in the same class,"

They all sat on a bench built under a mango tree that grew in the compound. "Jecinta!" her grandfather shouted her name. She had gone to the house to store away the basket that contained all the worldly possessions they owned. "Jecinta!" he called for the second time impatiently and in a voice heavy with authority. She came to know that grandfather was a man who would call out your name once and expect to see you before him almost instantly.

"Get some mangoes for the guests," she was ordered after emerging from the house. She was gone for quite a while but what she brought was a calabash of raw mangoes.

"Why are you offering them raw mangoes when we have ripe ones?" The old man had asked.

"I can't find any other," still in a sullen voice she answered.

"Please check in the giant pot," with patience, my grandfather requested. What she brought this time were mouth-watering ripe mangoes which they enjoyed.

Jecinta was the only daughter to their Aunt Rebecca and had lived all her life with her grandparents. With no other children in the home, she received all the love and attention that her grandparents had to offer. That evening, she realized that this privileged position was coming to an end with the arrival of the extra three children in 'her' home. This was not a very comfortable position and she saw them as a threat to her survival.

Her resentment was therefore instant and she could have done anything to send them back to the hole they came from. Unfortunately, this decision was not in her hands and all she could do was allow them in.

Not only was she to allow them into 'her home' but also move over a little and create space for the dirty-manure-smelling-girl on her bed! This was almost unimaginable and she was already thinking of how it would be later in the evening even before they took a second mango.

"Your grandmother went to the market but will be home soon. Meanwhile, Jecinta will show you around the village. I am off to see a neighbour but will be back after a short while," picking his hat from where it hung on a nail driven on the tree under which they sat, the old man picked his way out of the compound in his unhurried manner.

From what Ciku could remember from her last visit, *Guka* appeared to have changed little. Other than the baldness which had increased, everything else about him seemed the same. She could even have sworn that the hat he wore was the same old one. He was a man of average height but seemed taller because of the long trench coats he loved wearing.

Another thing she could have sworn about him is that his granary of stories was always loaded and that he never told a story twice. For all the time they spent with him in the last visit, he never retold a story. He had a new one any time they asked to be told a story.

Though he had changed a little, life was different and this is not the home Ciku had visited some years ago. In her last visit, *Guka* and his family lived on a farm which was some distance from Kandara shopping center. It was an organized compound with a fence and quite far from its nearest neighbour.

This new settlement was not a home but a prison in which each family had a cluster of huts. Like cows or goats or even chicken, the villagers were let out at six in the morning when the curfew ended, and were supposed to be in the compound by six in the evening when the curfew commenced. To ensure that no one sneaked in or out, the village was surrounded by a deep trench on whose floor was planted sharp wooden stakes .

The other person she could remember well from that visit was Jecinta. In those days she was a smallish fat girl with whom she had played a thousand games. All that had changed and she was no longer small and fat, but a thin girl taller than she was. The baby fat that had made her appear as if she could burst if pricked by a thorn was gone, leaving behind a mean tall girl. A girl with no time to spare for Ciku and her two brothers and only agreed to take them around the congested village simply because she had been ordered to.

Ciku had arrived looking forward to a good time with a cousin she had come to love in those days, a cousin who could have made her life easier and more enjoyable, especially after losing her parents. Instead what she saw on her face was far from love but hate. Raw hatred!

"My grandfather's homestead was nothing different from the other hundreds that dotted the *gicici* of Gakarara. It was made up of two huts, a granary and a roofless shed that served as the toilet. The biggest hut was occupied by my grandparents and Jecinta while the smaller one belonged to her uncle Mwirigi, the last born in her mother's family. Still unmarried, Mwirigi grazed the animals and was hard to find home at this time of the day."

"At the far end was a fenced-off area that secured the animals during the night. All the huts were hurriedly constructed and grass thatched. There was no fence separating different homesteads other that an open area of about ten meters. My mother, simply known as Ciku in those days, described the village her grandfather and everyone else had been forced to move to."

Three years ago, the colonial administration had ordered everyone to move from their ancestral land to the *gicici*. With everyone in the village, they effectively introduced a curfew which effectively cut off contact between the Mau Mau who operated during the night and the villagers.

"Ciku, our living arrangements are temporary. I think we will be back to our home in a few months," her grandfather had told her on seeing the surprise on her face. The hut they were to share with her grandparents and Jecinta was not very big and she doubted whether they would all fit in.

"But *Guka*, what happened to your old homestead?" Ciku had asked with concern.

Their old homestead was still intact but empty and desolate. It was overgrown with bushes and they would have to rebuild the houses when they went back. During the day, they cooked from the house as they worked on the farm but that was not enough to make it a home, her grandfather had informed her.

Gakarara village was located next to Gakarara Intermediate School and Ruchu Catholic Mission. Across the valley was the Kandara Shopping Centre. With a school, a dispensary, a shopping center, and a church nearby, the colonial government effectively controlled the local people. They worked on their farms during the day and by dusk everyone was indoors like chicken.

To secure the village during the night, the locals were forced to dig a trench all around it and plant the spear-like stakes. Recently, a child had died from injuries inflicted after accidentally falling into the trench while many more had been injured. The other major casualties were the animals.

The village had two entrances; the main gate that led to the school and the main road to Thika while the second entrance led to Thugi River from which they drew water. This was also the shortcut to Kandara Shopping Centre and the old villages.

Anyone returning home late was arrested and prosecuted while no one could leave the village during the curfew without the authority of the colonial D.O. based in Kandara.

Being led on a tour of such a village by a friendly person could have taken time for each homestead and structure had a story behind it, especially for children who were born in an urban center. In their case, things were different and her grandfather had not done a hundred steps before the tour came to an end at the very spot he had left them! Actually, it was not a tour because Jecinta had stood them at the center of the compound and pointed out the general location of the important landmarks around them.

"After the 'epic tour of the village', I sat back on the bench and at some point dozed off. The boys were busy playing a game of football using an empty can of the then-popular 'cowboy' cooking fat while Jecinta was busy doing her things in the house,"

"'You were sleeping so peacefully that I didn't want to disturb you', my grandmother who sat next to me on the bench, told me when I stirred from my sleep. I had not heard her return home and for how long she had sat by me could not tell," Ciku recounted of her meeting with her grandmother.

"Sorry *Cucu*, I did not sleep well last night,"

"I'm sorry for your troubles but you have been a

brave girl," she declared as she went to the house and came back with pieces of sugar cane which she distributed to Ciku and her brothers. Maria, Ciku's grandmother knew that it was almost impossible to talk while chewing a piece of sugar cane and therefore kept silent as the children enjoyed their chewing. She had removed the skin and even cut out the joints which are usually tough compared with the other part of the stem.

After clearing her share of the sugar cane, Ciku turned the hem of her dress and told her grandmother of the money hidden in it. She also disclosed that she had more cash hidden in the two dresses she wore and in the basket in which they had carried their belongings.

"Mom asked me to give you the cash," I told *cucu*.

"Going by the local standards, I would say that my grandmother was a tall lady though still shorter than my grandfather, a man of average height. You know men feel threatened by tall women and prefer marrying shorter women than they are,"

"They inherited their height from their mother who was a Maasai, a community whose people are generally of above average in height," Ciku, aka Wanjiku, my mother added while smiling at Julia my grandmother.

From where my mother got the notion that a woman ought to be shorter than the man she married for the matching of their heights to be perfect, I do not know. However I think it was foolish and one of the pillars that held high the superiority complex in men. Why a man shorter than his wife should feel threatened is beyond my understanding.

******

At the turn of the 19th century, the area around Ol Donyo Sabuk was devastated by tragedy after tragedy.

First to come was the rinderpest, a disease that within a short time wiped out almost the entire herd owned by the Maasai clan that grazed around the area. For a community whose main food was milk, blood, and meat, the loss of their animals was a threat to their very existence.

"Soon to follow was a famine that not only claimed the few animals that they still owned but members of the clan too. Children and the elderly were dying in numbers that left the community in shock," my grandmother, who had a moment ago once again taken over of the narration, told us.

She went on to narrate that bordering the traditional grazing land of the Maasai and beyond the Thika River was the land of the Agikuyu, a people who were successful tillers and keepers of animals. Their land was fertile and food was in plenty. From time to time, members of the two communities met while watering their animals on the banks of the river.

The Maasais would exchange ornaments with foodstuff like maize, beans, bananas, yams, and sweet potatoes which grew in abundance beyond the river. This trade grew bigger during famines. Rather than release the animals they held dear, the Maasai would instead offer their daughters for marriage in exchange for food. It was a cruel practice but the only way the community could be saved from hunger without releasing the few remaining animals for future breeding. This practice was common and not only brought food to hungry families but helped in easing the tension between the two communities.

To a people who spoke different languages and viewed each other with suspicion, deadly confrontations over pastures and use of the river used to occur from time to time. The Maasai, who believed that all the cows were originally theirs raided the land of the Agikuyu and carried away their animals. In retaliation, the Agikuyu would arrange a counter raid and they would as well carry away their animals and at times even young girls.

Their relationship since the occurrence of the deadly disease at the turn of the 19th century had greatly improved. This was because none of them dared graze their precious animals in a land believed to be cursed.

The land became wild and after several years all the traces that it had ever been habited were wiped out. This is the land that Macdonald, one of the early few white men to venture this far inland found. It was a land through which three major rivers with mighty waterfalls passed. He fell in love with it and would later encourage his fellow pioneer farmers to come and occupy. Their hunger for good land for farming was insatiable and kept their expansion program growing.

What they didn't know was that the empty land abundant with wild animals and suitable for farming was partly owned by the Agikuyu and that they would one day reclaim it with deadly results. The first crop they planted was sisal, a tough crop that could survive in the wilderness with little protection. Its thorny leaves kept away wild animals and no pest had interest in their fleshy leaves. Other crops like coffee soon followed and the need for more land to cultivate increased. Soon, the Agikuyu had nowhere to graze beyond their homesteads.

The theft of their land and the many oppressive rules that the colonialists imposed on the natives led to the formation of Mau Mau. Many of the first recruits to this organization were the jobless soldiers who had fought in the Second World War. They were experienced in modern warfare and easily forced the colonialists to their knees.

"Nyokabi, the great grandmother to my mother was one of those emaciated hungry Maasai girls who gallantly crossed the rivers ready for marriage to a strange people to save the rest of her families from hunger. In her company were a few elders who conducted the negotiations and the young men who carried back the foodstuff they bought. Nyokabi was bought by a cousin to the great Chief Karuri wa Gakure," my grandmother Julia told us.

As the pioneer farmers were busy grabbing tracts of land, the missionaries were in the quest of grabbing souls for Christ. The strange-looking men who spoke through their noses visited the Chief loaded with presents that he had never seen. These men who looked like butterflies were like no other medicine men and assenting to their simple request of setting a base in his area was easily granted. Tuthu, the home of Karuri wa Gakure became the first station of the Consolata Missionaries until they moved to Mathari in the present-day Nyeri. Under a tree, they established their first school and requested the chief to encourage his subjects to send their children.

Watiri, a girl born by a foreign woman and of little value in terms of dowry was one of the first pupils to be sent to this new school.

Shy, soft-spoken and fully aware of her inferior position in society, Watiri was an easy convert to Christianity. The love and respect she had never experienced in her home oozed in abundance from the strange-looking people.

The lessons were exciting and the girl was eager in learning the ways of the white man. Within a short period, she could write her name and understood a few English words.

In her fourth year of schooling, her ambition of excelling in education came to an end because her father wanted to raise dowry for one of the sons in his family. By giving Watiri out in marriage, the dowry he received in goats would cover part of the dowry. These were goats he needed desperately.

Watiri, now baptized Maria was torn between her

yearning for schooling and the handsome man selected for her for marriage. Not that she had any choice for a decision had already been made for her. After all, all her age mates were already married. Single and getting old left her in an awkward situation. She no longer fitted-in with her married friends, while those girls yet to be married were too young to associate with.

Mwangi the man she was to marry was a fellow school mate, and like a son to Karuri Wa Gakure. His real father was a fellow chief in one of the locations neighbouring Gakure.

My grandmother had come to the end of her narration of the deep history of my family but I was still confused. In my history lessons, I had learned of Karuri wa Gakure the dreaded colonial chief but did not know that I had ties with him. There were also other aspects of the story that needed clarification. An example was all the women she had mentioned.

"In summary, your mother Wanjiku is my daughter. Maria is me, the woman who was arrested in Naivasha and taken to detention. My mother was Watiri, one of the first pupils in the pioneer school in Tuthu. Watiri's mother and also my grandmother was Nyokabi, the Maasai girl sold to the Agikuyu," my grandmother Julia clarified.

Chapter Twelve

"The first sign that my brother Mwaniki was not well was a little coughing from time to time two days after our arrival. Though not alarming, it was a constant reminder of my mother's words that I should always keep him warm. The weather was sunny and I expected the coughing, now accompanied by sneezing, to go away in a few days. This didn't happen and by the end of the week, the simple flu had graduated into a wheezing chest and a constant flow of mucus," my mother narrated.

"I was worried, very worried once again."

The boy hardly ate and the medicine her grandfather prepared did little in controlling the flu. A boy who could have been busy running after goats and climbing the trees in the compound spent his day sleeping, delirious and crying for his mother. On her part, Ciku devoted her time to his care and she could have done anything to get him well. Together with her grandmother, they took him to the nearby Ruchu Mission Dispensary.

"What happened to this child?" The doctor who was an Italian nun wanted to know as she examined him. Her grandmother told of their arrival a week ago and of the night they spent on the road.

"Where did you spend the night?"

"In a police cell," Ciku answered.

"Was there a roof?"

"Yes"

"Where was that?"

"A place called Uplands. It was very cold,"

"No wonder then the boy fell sick. Uplands is not a place for children to spend the night in the open. I will raise a complaint with the D.O.," the doctor noted.

Dr. Marion had arrived at the clinic some two years earlier and though of European origin, she had grown popular with the local people for she was always kind and respectful to her patients. This was very different from the other white men who looked down on black people. She sent them away with some tablets and a bottle of drugs. "Come back in case he does not improve," she told them. Too weak to walk, they carried him back.

On the second night after the visit to the hospital, Mwaniki's sickness deteriorated. He was still very weak and had been eating very little. Though they kept him covered with layers of blankets, the boy was cold like someone freezing. His body shook and his teeth chattered.

Ciku was miserable as she watched him waste away while she could do nothing to save him. At about midnight, her grandmother strapped him to her back and together with her grandfather and Uncle Mwirigi sneaked out of the house headed to the dispensary. They found the guards on sentry duties warming themselves by a fire next to the gate.

"What do you want?" One of the guards asked with an unnecessary sternness.

"We are taking this child to the hospital," her grandfather explained.

"You know very well that we cannot allow you out of this gate at this time of the night?" Another guard informed them while shining his torch on the face of the sick child. By this time, all the guards were suspiciously standing around them. This could have been a feigned sickness and the purported sick child could have been a load of foodstuff or even guns for the Mau Mau.

"Afande, I know the rules but this child is seriously ill," her grandfather pleaded.

"Where were you during the day? You could have taken him to the hospital earlier,"

"Afande he was seen by Marion and she told us to go back in case he got worse,"

"That may be so but the rules remain the same. If our telephone was working, we could have called the boss and sought permission to let you out. But its dead," the guard who seemed to be the one in charge explained.

"Is there nothing you can do for us?"

"Nothing, go back and wait for the morning,"

Go back and wait till morning, with a child in a coma? Ciku wanted to shout back. Didn't they realize that her brother was dying? Tears of frustration swelled and freely flowed. What type of rules were those?

If there was ever a moment in her life when she felt raw anger directed at the white man and his supporters, this was it. Even the jailing of her parents was nothing compared with what was happening. If she had a gun, she could without any remorse have shot the guards down, opened the gate and proceeded to the hospital. She felt frustrated since she could do none of this. All she could do was cry her eyes out, while the boy slowly died. Defeated, her grandfather hushed her down as he led the way back to the house.

The arrest of her parents was a bad experience but there was an element of hope that maybe, they would be released later in the day, or if the worst came to the worst, after a few days. At some point, she even accepted their state of affairs and patiently waited. But to deny her sick brother access to a doctor was beyond what she could bear. All the energy to carry on was drained and her hope for the future crashed. Even walking back home was a problem and she had to lean on her grandfather.

"Ciku, things cannot continue like this. Our struggle for independence must continue with more urgency than ever before," *Guka* told her with bitterness after they were a distance from the guardhouse. At any other time, she could have had a comment to her grandfather's assertion but not tonight. The effort was too much. All she wanted was to get back into the house and sleep.

Back in the house, her grandmother placed Mwaniki on a mat and like before, covered him up. He continued shivering and deliriously talking to himself. Ciku squeezed herself on the mat he lay on and fell asleep almost immediately. The last thing she could remember was her grandmother sitting beside them and stoking the fire.

"Wake up, wake up!" she could hear the call but was too far away to respond.

"Wake up Ciku please, wake up," the calling continued. Slowly she came back from her dreamland. Together with her brothers and other children from their neighbourhood, were playing a game of hide-and-seek. It was her turn to find the children who hid in different corners of the compound by the time she opened her eyes. She located all the others but had trouble getting Mwaniki.

The setting was Naivasha though parts of the scenery appeared like their new home in Kandara. Some of the houses were made of mud and were grass thatched while she could also see the housing blocks they used to live in.

She had looked around all the buildings and the grounded train wagons parked behind their estate. She had even peered over the infamous trench in her new home but the boy was nowhere to be seen.

"Mwaniki, Mwaniki," she had continuously called with no response.

"Mwaniki, Mwaniki, the game is over and you are the winner," still no response.

The other children joined her in calling the boy but he was nowhere. They were about ten in number and they divided themselves into two groups and searched in different directions.

Ciku was getting anxious over what had happened to him. What if he had fallen in the well behind the sheds?"

"Ciku, Ciku," her grandmother who had joined the search called. She headed towards the direction of her voice. Slowly she came from sleep to the call of her grandmother.

Even without opening her eyes, she could tell that the sun was shining brightly.

"How did you sleep?" Her grandmother enquired when she saw her stir. She grunted some answer with her mind far away to the game they had been playing. "Where is Mwaniki?" She asked with anxiety and guilt for not only sleeping the whole night without checking on him but for sleeping late. Even with the loving care they received from her grandparents, she still felt that looking after her brothers, especially the sick one, was her primary responsibility.

"His condition has improved. He even took some porridge and did not vomit," as if a heavy load was removed from her shoulders, she felt a relief that made her crash back onto her sleeping mat.

"Where is he?"

"He is basking in the sun."

After a moment, she rose to a sitting position with an intention of joining Mwaniki. Strangely, the task left her panting and her head throbbing as if in her head, a thousand drummers competed. She once again slumped back on the mat panting and sweating. All she wanted was to lie down and just rest.

"Are you well?" Her grandmother asked with concern.

"I feel as if I am having malaria,"

"Sorry, can I get you anything?"

"Maybe some water," she told her in a weak voice.

Later, she pushed herself into taking some porridge

but she vomited almost immediately. These were the symptoms that her brother had shown a week ago. Without delay, she was taken to the dispensary by her grandmother and was given some drugs.

Even after the visit to the dispensary, she felt no better and suspected that the medication that was prescribed made her feel even worse. For the next week or so, the only thing that her stomach could hold was water, while all she wanted to do was sleep.

For the first time, in her life, she had dreams that were so real that she could not tell where reality ended and the dreaming started. One dream would easily merge with the next one, and she could even pause from a dream when she arose from sleep, and later continue from where she had stopped.

In one of the dreams which took more than a day, she saw neighbours sitting outside their house when she came back from school. What's wrong? She wanted to shout from afar.

She did not have long to wait and with an animal-like piercing voice, wailed. The last thing she could remember of that evening was grasping her friend's hand because her legs were slowly turning into reeds, and were too weak to carry her weight. In one moment, she was standing upright, and in the next, she was lying on the dusty floor. In the dream, they must have carried her into the house and laid her on a mat. She arose to find her new friend Wanjugu sat beside her, wearing a sad face.

"Have I slept for long?" She asked.

"Not very long but you should now wake up,"

"I will but give me a few minutes." The dream continued.

She needed to think and review a few things. Her major worry was that she had failed her mother. What will she say when she comes back?

In her long dream, they buried her brother that afternoon at her *Guka's* old homestead of Kiriko-ini. A grave had been dug and all the necessary burial papers prepared. A stretcher for carrying the body had been made by piercing an old gunny bag with two long sharp poles on its two long edges. Looking at the boy, he appeared as if he was peacefully sleeping. Earlier on, she had shaken his shoulder just to make sure that he was truly dead and that no one had made a mistake.

There was no response; Mwaniki was dead, she continued dreaming.

They dressed him in a pair of shorts and a flowery shirt that he loved wearing when going for the Sunday service. As a way of making him opt for another shirt, they used to skip washing it while doing his other clothes or made sure it was wet on Sunday morning.

He lay on his back, rigid as if he was playing the game of statue. In this game, if your partner said the word "statue" you are expected to freeze in whatever pose you were in. If you had your hands in the air, that's where they are supposed to remain with the rest of your body frozen in whatever position it was in, until you were told to relax.

As for her brother, it was as if somebody had said the word statue while he was lying down but forgot to tell him 'relax'. Thus like a statue, he rigidly continued sleeping.

That morning Ciku wept over a boy who was a brother, a friend and a son all rolled together. A boy who should not have died! She also wept over her parents who were detained in a land far away without trial over imaginary crimes against the racist white masters, and denied the right to even bury their child.

She cried with bitterness over the white masters who not only denied her brother the right to be cared for by his parents but also denied them the right to take him to the hospital. Whether he could have survived or not did not matter. All she knew is that he was dead after being denied permission to be taken to the hospital.

"I will revenge for you my brother," in her dream, Ciku made a solemn vow silently while placing her hand on his chest.

The procession that bore his body moved in a single file down the treacherous slope towards Thugi River, past Kandara Shopping Centre up to her grandfather's old home. Pastor Wanjingiri from the Independent Church, then a young man, conducted the brief ceremony. All through, she remained calm but worried over the future of her brother. Though dead, there was a part of her that still thought that he needed her care. What was going to happen to him when they returned home and left him in this lonely grave? The Pastor had an answer.

"Father, we are going back to *gicici* and will leave your son alone. My prayers are that you send an angel to guard this grave until the day you come back blowing a trumpet for the dead to rise. I also pray that you will send another angel to look after these children who have lost their brother. Give them solace that you alone can provide. We also remember the parents of this child, wherever they are this afternoon take care of them.............Amen."

The prayers were not consoling and made no sense at all and Ciku wondered why a whole angel would spend time guarding a grave while he could have guarded the boy against death? What she would have liked God to do was first to bring back her brother to life. After all, she had learned at an early age that God was all-powerful!

The other thing she would have liked Him to do was to punish the angel who had 'slept on his job' and allowed this death. Without doing these two things everything else was illogical and for the second time, the foundation of her faith was badly shaken. The dream continued.

In her Sunday school class, she was also taught that God was ever loving and almighty. Where was His love when He allowed the white man to take both her parents away?

Her soul was empty and didn't know where to turn to for comfort. That 'night', as she lay on her mat ready to sleep, she didn't know what to tell a God who was a disappointment on so many occasions, a God who was no longer loving and compassionate. She lay awake for a long time with her mind moving from one thing to the next. Besides her but on another mat was Jecinta, snoring. She was disgusted that she could snore as she always did even when her brother lay alone in that cold and dark grave.

She knew that she was being unreasonable because the rest of the family was asleep as well but she needed to vent her anger on someone.

Deep in some compartment of her heart, she knew that God was able to make right all the things which were going wrong in her life. She also knew that she had no way of knowing what was happening to her parents other than praying that God may keep them safe. All of a sudden she realized that she still needed God more than at any other time in her life. She needed Him to keep safe the remaining members of her family.

With this realization, she turned to God with a new understanding and prayed, "God you are still out there and am sorry for doubting your presence around me in the last one month, hear my prayers. Do not allow the angel of death near us and keep my parents safe wherever they are."

It took her maybe an hour or so to determine whether she was asleep or awake. In between, she dozed and awoke. She could not concentrate on anything without dozing off at some point and she would pick up her thinking all over again. It was a struggle but she could vividly remember every step of her dream from the start. Could the arrest of her parents and their subsequent movement to Kandara be a part of the long dream? Was her brother dead and buried? Everything was confusing and muddled up.

She stretched her hand to the space she last left her brother sleeping beside her but there was nothing. No warm body but the rough dusty feel of the earthen floor beyond the mat. The rough floor removed the possibility that she was in their smooth floored house in Naivasha.

Though assured, moments of doubt still crept into her mind. What if they had spent the day burying her brother? Her heart missed a beat. What if she was still asleep and dreaming that her brother was dead? This took her back to where she was a moment ago.

She tried to sit up but the effort was too much. Her legs were too heavy and all her joints felt jelly-like. She turned her head and faced the direction of the door which was open and shed light to the room. The action was also too hard for her and sent a wave of sweating on her brows. The light was blinding and she could see nothing definite other than blurring rays of the sun.

At some point, she heard footsteps approaching the house and in a moment a dark outline of a person framed the entrance. Who it was, she couldn't tell and bothered not. She must have closed her eyes for a moment because when she refocused on the door again, the figure was gone. Frantically, she wanted to shout to whoever it was to come back but her dry throat failed her. For the first time since she woke up, she felt thirsty and desperately needed a drink.

She must have fallen back to sleep for the next thing she felt was a soothing touch of something wet and cool passing over her face. She could also hear voices though they sounded very far away and faint.

"She was awake a moment ago," a voice that sounded familiar declared. With a feeling of success, she realized that the voice belonged to Jecinta. This was a breakthrough in her reawakening process. For the first time since they arrived from Naivasha, she was experiencing tenderness from Jecinta. This was confusing but at the same time enjoyable.

Face mopping was set aside and while holding her head from behind, a soothing cup of water was held onto her lips. The first swallow was sweeter than honey and more satisfying than anything she had ever tasted.

Later, she heard from Jecinta how sick she had been for the last two weeks. She had slept late in the morning of the night they were sent back with her sick brother but none was bothered for she was yet to start schooling. Her sleeping raised an alarm when Muna tried to wake her up at around ten in the morning and got no response. He ran to her grandmother claiming that Ciku was ignoring him and had refused to wake-up.

On realizing that Ciku was very sick and too weak to walk her grandmother called a neighbour who assisted in carrying her to the dispensary. Malaria and typhoid tests were conducted but the results were negative. Dr. Marion was surprised for she could not diagnose her ailment. She was given some tablets which she was forced to swallow in between her never-ending sleep.

As Jecinta narrated about her sickness, there was one worrying question she still feared asking. Her fears were not in the asking but in the answer she could get. Where is Mwaniki?

She wanted desperately to ask.

Mwaniki's entrance into the room saved her but it also raised doubts on whether what she saw was a ghost or not. Not sure that she could still speak, she beckoned Mwaniki with her hand and indicated that he should sit down beside her. When he sat, she stretched her hand and patted him as she reassured herself that this was not a ghost but her brother.

She was overjoyed on realizing that Mwaniki was not dead and all along she had been in a long delirious dream. He had been sick, yes, but his healing marked the start of her ailment.

"Your breathing was less labored and the sweat that had drenched your body was now evaporated," my grandmother continued with the narration.

Her wrinkled face with the eyes sunken deep in the sockets was heavy with emotion. The scene she was describing was unfolding afresh in her mind and it was as if she was alone with the sick girl.

Chapter Thirteen

"She returned home from detention almost a year later," my mother said pointing at Julia, her mother and my *shosh*. "By then I had fully recovered from my sickness and could say that I had never felt better health-wise," my mother continued with her face lit by the embers of the dying fire.

At a distance, maybe in the next compound, we could hear the ominous cries of the owl which sent shivers in the rather quiet night. It was a bad omen for an owl to cry from your compound. It is believed that someone was going to die in the family. This fear became acute if a member of that family was sick.

In that year, her mother was away, all the children were enrolled at Gakarara Intermediate School and for a girl who liked learning, catching up with the rest of her classmates was easy. Slowly but steadily, she 'climbed' from the bottom to be among the top ten performers in her class. Her aim was to attain position one.

Like on any other day, she was walking home with her friend Wanjugu who lived some three homes from her. This was one part of the day she used to enjoy and they would chat and chat until they got home.

"I saw you with a pile of books headed to the teachers' quarters," her friend commented.

"Oh, those were Mr. Karunde's," Mr. Karunde was their mathematics teacher and lived in the school compound.

"Be careful, he has a habit of doing things to girls," "He didn't do anything to me. I left him in the staffroom when I did the delivery,"

"That is how it starts. Next time he might set the

delivery in a way that you will find him home,"

"He does not appear evil and has been very helpful in making sure that I catch up with the rest of the class,"

"I am just telling you to be alert. Right now he is like a cat whose paws are so soft you would think that it has no claws,"

"I also have claws and I can claw back,"

"You are joking. That is not the way to do it. By the time you claw back a baby will be on your hands. The easiest way to fight back is to avoid entering his house on your own. Any time he sends you to the house, make sure that you are in the company of another person, never alone!"

"Ooh, I now understand,"

"Do you know Njoroge's sister?"

"Which Njoroge?"

"The one in our class,"

"I know her. The one with a new baby?"

"Yes, that one. The baby is a result of a book delivery,"

"In that case, I will refuse to take the books,"

"You cannot do that. He will punish you or even find a reason to beat you up. Just make sure that you are not alone with him. For a girl to survive the men and boys who are more than friendly, one has to be wise,"

"Madam Counselor, what do I do with boys who refuse to release my hand after a handshake?" She jokingly asked.

"Aaa. Those are easy to handle, push them away," she advised laughingly.

"What about those who try touching private parts?"

"If anybody touches any part of your body that is private, push him away and scream. If he persists, learn how to say no, a big NO that will attract attention. Such a NO will scare him off. It will also send a loud and clear message that what he is doing is wrong. If you do it immediately and in the open, the better. The news will spread to the other boys and they will be respectful when dealing with you or with any other girl. Remember to report the incident to the nearest teacher,"

"How do you know all these things?"

"My mother tells me."

"Oooh," she answered in a lame voice. The mention of her mother changed her mood. How she would love to have her mother back!

"Ciku, I am sorry about your parents. I pray for you every night," she consoled.

"Thank you, my friend. I do not know how I could have survived their absence without the support of people like you. You have shown me love and made my stay in school easy,"

"I wish there was anything better I could do for you. All I can do is to offer my friendship."

Emotionally they embraced as they parted near her home and she walked on for the next few meters thinking of her parents. She missed her mother. From her science lessons, they had learned that a woman carries a baby in her womb for nine months. From her estimate, her mother should have delivered by now and the baby could be around eight months or so. How was she? How was the baby? Is it a boy or a girl? How she wished the baby to be a girl. It would balance-off the equation in her family.

For a moment, she thought that she was seeing a vision. In front of the house was her mother in the same maternity dress she wore on the day of her arrest. She could not believe her eyes. She dropped her school bag and dashed into her open arms.

"It is hard to express my feelings at that moment with words. It was a feeling of joy beyond description. My heart was beating at a rate beyond limit while I cried with joy. I closed my eyes and clung to my mothers' embrace," she narrated.

"After what appeared like a hundred years of embrace, I let her loose and holding me at an arms' length with both hands, she inspected my face,"

"I am more than joyful to see you, my dear," her mother declared. Ciku could get no words out of her chest to respond to her mum's comments. It was as if she was choking from a big bite of boiled sweet potato.

"I missed you mum," she whispered with tears streaming down her face.

"Don't cry my dear, rejoice that I am back."

Ciku left her for a while as she picked her school bag from where she had thrown it and then went into the house and changed from her uniform. On coming back, she carried a stool and sat across her mother.

"Tell me how you are doing Ciku. How is the new school?" There was so much she wanted to know.

"I am enjoying the new school and the teachers and my fellow pupils are very kind to me,"

She told her of their journey, Mwaniki's sickness and the cruelty of the guards in preventing them from taking him to hospital.

"Do you know I almost died of Malaria?"

"Sorry dear!"

"I was sick for two weeks. No eating, just sleeping. I was too weak to even visit the toilet,"

"God is great you are now well. I was praying for you every day,"

"I also prayed for you mum. How have you been?" What she wanted to know was where the baby was, but had no way of asking directly. After all, they had never spoken over the expected baby before her arrest. Not that there was need for such talk because her ballooning tummy announced loudly of its coming.

Her mother's face clouded as she remembered her experiences since the time of her arrest. She was thinner than she used to be and the maternity dress hung very loose over her slim body. Maybe it is the maternity dress, the dress she had worn when heavy with a baby that made her appear thinner than she was.

"Ciku my experiences in jail were horrifying and I do not want to burden you with the details. I was tortured, kept hungry until I lost the baby. It was a painful experience but God kept me from death," she painfully narrated.

"Sorry mum,"

"Don't worry over me. The important thing as of now is that I am back and you are all safe,"

"Have you ever heard anything about Dad?"

"Nothing Ciku. My daily prayer is that he is well."

Her grandfather had gone to the farm and he was yet to return while her grandmother had gone to the river with Jecinta and her two brothers. They heard their approach even before they arrived in the compound. Her grandmother and Jecinta carried jerry cans on their backs while the two boys carried small ones with their hands.

"When they saw me, the boys dropped their water cans and rushed to my arms. On their part, your grandmother and Jecinta went on and poured the water into the drum while the jerry cans were still on their backs. Then they came over and hugged me," Julia, my grandmother told us of her homecoming reception.

"Mum, you see I have grown strong and can even carry a big water can," Muna boasted.

"Me too mum, I assist *cucu* in drawing water," Mwaniki interrupted even before his mum commented.

"I can see that you have grown big and strong. I believe that *cucu* has been busy feeding you," Julia complimented them.

Chapter Fourteen

With her mother around, time flew in a way she could not understand and in a few weeks, the year was coming to an end and she was soon going to sit for her Common Entrance Examination. This was the examination she had missed after their displacement from Naivasha and was sat in class four.

She was still worried about her father who had been away for more than a year but sort of got used to his absence. I guess that is what happens when you lose a loved one. You mourn and miss him for a time but somehow get used to his or her absence. You no longer think of the deceased every moment because there are so many things happening around you, and life has to go on.

"I sat for my Common Entrance Examination and when the results came out got a sweet surprise. My performance was far better than my expectations and I was admitted to the next level of education which was class five to class eight where Kenya African Preliminary Examination (KAPE) was administered. I did well in my KAPE and was admitted to Kahuhia High School. Life in high school was fun though the studies were at times tough. I do not intend to tire you with the day to day details," Ciku, summarized her schooling life.

"Just after my exams, we received our independence and everybody was excited and happy. However, I regretted that I didn't get an opportunity to revenge as I had always wanted. However, I consoled myself with the fact that not everyone had to go to the forest to fight. There were many other ways in which one could have contributed to the struggle. For instance, I had taken care of my brothers while my parents were in jail. That was my role in the struggle though what I could have enjoyed most was seeing the face of a white police officer as I caused him pain for his mistreatment of my parents,"

"The other major turning point in my life was my admission to Thogoto Teachers College after Kahuhia," she continued.

"The college admitted students from all over the country and you can imagine my surprise when I met Otieno, your father," my mum touched on a subject that most interested me. Why had she married so far away from her home? I always wanted to know.

The student population was large and she did not get into meeting him until her second term in the college and it took a lot of courage. Otieno was a son to their neighbour, Mama Akinyi in Naivasha. She last saw him on the day his mother packed *nguja gutu* for them in readiness for their departure. He had grown into a tall handsome young man and she could not have recognized him had it not been for the letters.

All the letters for the students were given out during the evening parade. "John Munene, Edwin Otieno, Naomi Njoroge, Prisca Mutua, etc." the one distributing the letters would call out.

The name Edwin Otieno sounded familiar but she could not remember where she had heard of it. Every time the name was called, she would reprimand herself for having no courage of approaching the tall young man who responded to the name.

"Excuse me, have we met?" One day she gained courage and asked.

"I think so. I have been seeing you since last term. You are in your first year aren't you?" He asked with a knowing smile.

"Yes but that's not what I meant. Had we ever met before I came here?"

"I don't think. Why do you ask?"

"Your name sounds familiar,"

"Some names are similar,"

"Have you ever lived in Naivasha?"

"Naivasha? Yes, that is where I grew up. Why do you ask?"

"My family lived in Naivasha as well,"

"Sure?"

"Yes. Do you know a lady we used to call Mama Akinyi? Her husband worked with the railways?" She saw the surprise on his face. Could this be Mama Akinyi's son? A boy who was older than her friend Akinyi? It was getting interesting.

"Yes, that is my mother,"

"*Wa wa waa*, then we were neighbours. I am Ciku,"

"Ciku! The girl I knew has grown up into something. *Wa*! I couldn't have recognized you at all!"

"Me too, you are quite different from the boy I knew,"

"Where have you been?"

"We went back to our rural home and continued growing and schooling. Here I am now," she said conversationally.

"How are your parents? Were they ever released?"

"My mother was released after one year. But my father......" she had paused, sadness of losing her father clouding an otherwise happy moment.

"What happened?"

"We were informed by his fellow prisoner a year before independence that he was a victim of a cholera outbreak in Manyani. That must have been in his first year of imprisonment,"

"I am so sorry Ciku, really sorry," he paused. "Your family vanished from this earth with no trace. My mother still keeps a black box that contains some of your things,"

"Sure, my mum will be delighted to hear that,"

It was on a weekend with no pressing business to attend to for the two old neighbours and they spent the better part of the afternoon chatting over the olden days. She came to know that Akinyi was married years earlier and lived in Siaya, while his father had retired and retreated to their rural home.

Naturally, she invited him for a visit to their home when they broke out for their half-term vacation.

When Otieno went home for the next holiday, he pulled from their store the old black wooden box, which was popularly known as Baba Ciku's box. It was still locked and the key kept by his father. Everyone in the family knew of its history and his father used to say that his one wish before he died was to deliver it to its rightful owners. Unfortunately, he was transferred to Kisumu abruptly before he could fulfil this desire.

When their household property was loaded into the cargo train headed to Kisumu, Baba Ciku's box was among them. Though they were moving in the opposite direction from Baba Ciku's home, Baba Akinyi's intention of one day delivering the box was not dimmed. He still believed that Baba Ciku would be released from the detention soon, and that he would come looking for him. This did not happen and when he retired, the box was once again among the items loaded into the lorry headed to their rural home in Seme.

Deep in Baba Akinyi's heart, there was still a flicker of hope that somehow he would deliver the box to Baba Ciku's family wherever they were. It was therefore not a complete surprise when Otieno brought him the news that they were in the same college with Ciku. He was pleased that they were well but saddened by the death of his old colleague and neighbour.

In a letter during the holiday, Otieno informed Ciku

that he would be travelling back using an overnight OTC bus from Siaya. Ciku and her mum, therefore, met him at the OTC bus terminus where the handing over of the box was done.

"The box was heavy but I had brought a rope with which I tied it up and carried it on my back. When I got home and on opening it, I wept as I went through its contents," Grandmother Julia who had taken over the narration told us in her melodious voice.

"In the box, I found that old radio," she told us while pointing at the old radio that sat on the table.

"The iron box we use was also there, family portraits, your grandfather's clothes, my clothes, their clothes were also there," She paused as she pointed with her scrawny finger at my mum.

"Also in the box was my wedding dress which lay at the bottom just as I had packed it with our marriage certificate tucked in one of its folds. Among the portraits was that of our wedding day which now hangs on the wall of the living room. There was also a file that contained correspondence between your grandfather and his employer and important family documents,"

"What about the bicycle and the sewing machine?" I asked her.

"Oh, I was forgetting about them. They were delivered but on another trip."

In that second trip, Otieno brought the bicycle and the sewing machine. This time, Ciku was with Muna who tied-up the sewing machine on the carrier and rode the bicycle home. "I gave the bicycle to Muna who to this day, still use it. For the sewing machine, I gave it to Mwaniki when he married," she continued.

That old sewing machine was still in use in Auntie Elsa's tailoring shop located in Kandara shopping center. Elsa was Uncle Mwaniki's wife. "I still have the box and it still contains many of the old things. Their old clothes, and all the things I had no use of are still there. Remind me to show you the contents tomorrow," Julia concluded the story of the old box.

* * * * * *

"That is how I met your father," my mum declared with pride.

"That's a moving story,"

"It is Becky and I can still remember a question you asked and no one answered on the day we escaped from Kisumu," she reminded me.

"You asked, will I ever go back to Kisumu?"

"Yes, I do remember,"

"Kisumu and in particular Seme is where your umbilical cord was buried. It is also where your father is buried. These are links you can never sever. Kisumu is your home regardless of what some people did to you,"

"What are you telling me, Mum?"

"I am telling you that running away from Kisumu is running away from your past. You can't run away from your past and if you do, it will always haunt you,"

"What do I do?"

"For your own sake, forgive those who have wronged you," "Mum that's asking too much. How do I forgive those who killed our friends and burned our houses?"

"You have to Becky. Not everyone was involved in torching our home. Many people have been very kind and loving to us. Do you want to condemn them with those criminals? You cannot do that. Remember, there are good members of the Kikuyu community just as there bad members among them. There are also good members of the Luo community just as there are bad ones among them. There are good Kambas, Kalenjins, Luhyas, Maasais and many other tribes, but among them there are few bad people."

"It is the same with religion. For instance, there are good Christians and bad Christians. There are also good Moslems and bad Moslems. The bad ones are Christians or Moslem by name only. They are people who are evil more than the heathens and give religion a bad name,"

"This is why you can't condemn a whole community just because there are some bad elements among them," my mum concluded.

"It's hard,"

"Did I say it's easy? I didn't. For you to be a truly great woman, you have to start doing things differently. By forgiving others, you remove yourself from the level of the person you are forgiving. You start operating at a higher level. You gain a new understanding," she was quiet for a moment.

"I see Mum. I do forgive them for they knew not what they were doing."

THE END

SOON TO BE RELEASED

Waters of Joy
By Andrew Maina

Synopsis

During a raid to their manyatta by some Agikuyu tribesmen, Sakunda, a Maasai girl is abducted. She is moved to a strange land, given a new name and gifted as a wife to one of the warriors who participated in her abduction. In accepting him as a husband, she extracts a solemn vow that he would one day take her to the land she was born for a visit.

With children to raise and a husband she has come to love, Sakunda, whose new name is Nyokabi puts on hold her desire of visiting her homeland for many seasons. When she finally makes the visit, she finds her ailing mother alone for her two sisters are already married, while her father and brother are dead.

She also finds alive the old man to whom she was to be married in a deal struck long before she was born. He is still waiting though ailing and half blind. This man who was older than her father, questions the legitimacy of her marriage to the man in her company, but reluctantly agrees to accept the refund of the dowry he paid a long, long, time ago.

Njamba, her Kikuyu husband, the man who abducted her but she now loves, is forced to go back for the animals with which he is to pay the dowry demanded.

One of the elders who claim to have seen Njamba during the raid in which many were killed, and their animals stolen, sends two warriors to follow and kill him.

This mission fails and Njamba manages to find his

way home only to find that most of his livestock died from a strange disease while he was away. Devastated, he gives up hope of immediately reclaiming Nyokabi and embarks on rebuilding his wealth.

After waiting for many seasons for the promised dowry refund, the Maasai elder demand Sakunda for a wife. She is outraged and rather than wait for a forced marriage to an old man she loathes, Nyokabi escapes to the land of the Agikuyu. She tearfully escapes to a man, to a land and to a people she once hated but now love.